ZOESIS

Zoesis

by Jim Marcus

February 2025

This book is set in Lato Regular 9/13
Titles in Lato Heavy 16/20

Cover:
Rebirth

by Jim Marcus 2025

Edited by
Reed Floarea

979-8-9924718-0-9

Chapters

Zoesis n. [zhōh-ēs-əs]

A point in an organism's development where they are optimized for life : of or relating to that stage in a lifecycle: LIVING, VITAL

The Accident

When I was younger, I always thought I would die in some spectacularly fun way.

Like, I'd be having athletic sex with two hot people on the back of some kind of previously uninvented experimental flying machine, and I'd be in the middle of "climax", which is what the YA adventure books I read called it, and we'd hit, like, a bird or something, and I would go flying and, for one split second, just for a moment, naked, propelled forward, some homemade buttplug, slammed up inside me, feeling like I was flying, and I'd put my arms in front of me, and open my eyes as wide as they got, and splat, hit a mountain or something, buttplug still in view of everyone.

And ghost me would hold up a "10" card or something, and applaud and be like, "Well done, little bitch, you died the best".

And there would be the funeral and everyone would go into detail at the event about what a great big whore I was. Oh, of course I was a good person and they all loved me. But they would play that final footage, and everyone would see me getting off and then, immediately after dying, my ass on display for everyone. They would go into detail about how I was one of the greatest fucks of their lives, and talk about the little things I did, that no one else would do, because I was just that dirty.

My funeral would be this big orgy and I would be on display, still naked and all the people there would be like, "Man, I'd love the chance to just rail her one last time," and maybe some of them would because I'd leave behind a will that said it was ok. "You can grieve by getting your rocks off in me."

It would say. The legal document.

And that would go on for days.

Given that fantasy, I'm not sure what pisses me off more, that I don't remember the accident at all, or that I'm twenty-four now and still a massive untouched virgin.

So, maybe I have time to get that final will notarized.

When I was 12, apparently, I had an accident. It fucked with my memory a bit. So, I don't really remember it. It wasn't epic, but it may have involved some government service, so, because my family had a really good lawyer, I got this settlement. Explaining it would be pretty complicated, but my accountant says that I could spend about 50,000 dollars a day and still only be spending the interest. So, it's not a trust fund, it's a THRUST fund.

I use that joke all the time and no one laughs but me.

I don't know if I was having fun. I'm guessing I wasn't because there is really only so much fun a twelve year old can have. And, in all honesty, my aspirations toward being a giant slut were probably tempered by what it means to be a young girl. It's all still deeply intertwined with, well, just being liked.

My 12 year-old girl brain parsed sex as "I will feel good and people like me." Nothing further than that, really. At that age, it's about being someone's PERSON- the thing they think about. Sometimes when you're a kid you feel like you don't exist when no one is thinking about you. But you might not know what it means when they are.

My brain was never really the same after the accident. I still think about sex all the time.

And I mean, all the time. And if you have a problem with that, stop reading my journal right now, perv. What the fuck.

You gone? Good.

But there is a lot wrapped up in that. I also have trouble really losing weight. For the last five years or so - since I was about 19 - I've been 5'4" and 200 pounds and neither of those dimensions is changing anytime soon. I don't think I'm large, but I'm keenly aware of what the media thinks about all this. More than that, I grew up immersed in what men think about it.

They're probably the same thing. The Media. Men.

But men love to tell you what's acceptable.

The biggest problem, though, is what I call RAS - Rejection Amplification Syndrome. This is my life, so, again, if you don't want to know, get the fuck out of my diary, sherlock.

It's kind of fun kicking you fuckers out. Andele.

Anyway. Let's say you are a woman living on earth at any time in history. This exact time, for the record, is March 15th, 2499. We're about 9 months away from a major round number and everyone is going a little nuts. All of the following still applies, though.

You are a woman. At some point after you are born, sometimes very soon after you are born, men begin to notice you as "a thing they can have sex with™."

So they try. It doesn't matter who you are or what you look like, they will try. If you're shaped like a box, they will try to find a hole in that box. If you are naturally in some gaseous state they will learn chemistry to turn you material again. If you are six hundred feet tall, they will put on their climbing shoes and dig in. If you are locked in a tin can, they will invent the can opener.

You get it.

They may act nice, they may act like it's a joke, they may act romantic, but it will happen. It's a universal law.

They will make a move.

And you will say yes or no.

If you say yes, and continue saying yes forever and ever, you will have no problem. You are both on the train together. You can drive off into the sunset. That train will chug along nicely.

Here's what happens when you say no.

The brain shrivels up into a tiny hard object and it launches insults, attacks, disdain, consequences, really anything it can at you. That is sort of universal. And people can say "not all men," but it's enough men that people nod when you say it.

Here's where my weight factors in.

The optimum weight for me is 120 pounds. Now, when a man hits on you, and you reject him, for every ten pounds over that you are, he levels up one anger notch. It's just math. So the larger you are, even though you know you're attractive and desirable, the more you keep your head down sometimes.

Because that's a lot of anger notches.

Was it RAS that's kept me from fucking my way across the country? I don't know. All I know is that if I think about actual penetrative sex in the abstract, I get wet like a magnificent lake full of lakewater and just general lake stuff. But if I get close to actually *doing* it, I dry up like a tardigrade and float away on the next big wind.

I'm going to go back later and update those analogies. Probably.

***

"Are you writing about the accident again?" Meijo tried to read over my shoulder.

"No. It's a hard-boiled detective novel." I lied.

"uh-huh. " Rik cut in. Do you know that when you two don't hit a button at all, I just win. Automatically. Like I don't even need to be good at this." Rik was apparently the only one still playing the game of Krakoa, a new game we just got where you try to fuck the world up as bad as you can before the giant underground volcano eradicates you. It's a little dark. My game model is really unregulated capitalism. That always ends with slavery, high priced breathable air, and zombie chemical agents in the water supply.

"I wish I could play as the volcano. Fuck you people up." Meijo was my best friend. He might have been my boyfriend. I really didn't know. If you asked him, he would tell you he has forgotten where his apartment is, so that makes him officially my boyfriend. His hair was dark like mine, but while I'm Cuban, he's Dominican. So it's totally different. He weighed about 120 soaking wet and was not too much taller than me. Most people would have guessed he was gay at first glance, but he was sort of an all around kind of guy and, honestly, in my mind, an exception to all the bad things I could ever say about men.

Rik, on the other hand, WAS pretty much totally gay. I'm the only girl he ever played with at all and I swear he just closed his eyes. He was a giant, handsome black man and we'd been friends for almost ten years now. Rik was gathering his stuff up to leave.

This was my group, my coven. My people.

"Can I suck your dick before you go?" I crawled over to him.

"Ordinarily, I might be inclined to say yes, but I have a big thing in the morning." Rik had an actual job. He ran the technology department of a whole school. So, yes, maybe important. i thought about making a joke out of "big thing"

"Damn students." I pouted.

"Yes, dear, I say that every day." Rik gave me a quick kiss and ran off down the hall toward the door.

"He's taking his dick with him." Meijo sat back down and picked up the controller. The game wasn't as much fun alone. It was just like, "hey, let's break shit." Which works, I guess.

He leaned back into the chair and spread his legs just a little. I crawled over to him and put my head in his lap. Meijo had been really patient with me. We'd been hanging out for almost five years now and i'd never let him fuck me. We still had fun. But I swear, it did feel like his openness was making it easier for me to get to the next place. A place where I, hopefully could be me.

I liked sucking someone off while they were doing something fun. Meijo was always good about making it last, and paying just enough attention to me for me to feel like he was loving it, but not so much that it felt like I wasn't just a total whore.

I ran my face over the bulge between his legs. I tried to feel his cock through the thin fabric of his shorts. I could feel him getting harder the wetter I made them. I opened my mouth wide and fit the entire bulge in my mouth, feeling him move his hips a little to accommodate me.

When he lifted his hips a little from the chair, I pulled the shorts down and off over his feet. His legs were still slightly spread so I was able to slide my mouth in around his balls and suck them one at a time. I loved having him in my mouth, feeling the slight hair on his balls against my face. I wondered if I could have gotten both his and Rik's cock in my mouth at the same time. I'd never tried that but it seemed like I could. My mouth was wet and mobile and soft and I licked up the shaft of his prick and let my tongue sit in the groove under the head.

I crawled under his leg and spread him wider so I could get my mouth all the way down his dick from the front. His was smaller than Rik's but it had a really pretty shape and I felt that sense of accomplishment from getting the whole thing in my mouth and down my throat. I tried to imagine myself as a sucking machine, a toy that would totally encompass how prick and let him do what he needed to do. His little moans were coming now, alongside the running conversation with the game.

I waited until he started pumping a little and then held his ass with both hands and tried to match his rhythm.

Finally, his hand came down on my head and he pushed down hard. I felt the little pop of his cock head in the back of my throat and made sure my mouth was wet. He pumped at my face, holding my head with both hands now. I could hear the game stalling as he bucked harder and harder, shoving his pretty dick into the space in my throat I made for him. I heard that noise he makes when he is starting to get ready and tried my best to match the rhythm. It felt like a beat to me. So many dongs I could hear in my head with that speed, that rhythm, in and out, just pumping. My mouth started to feel like it didn';t belong to me anymore. I fantasized that I wasn't moving, just he was.

And as he got closer, the salty, alkaline taste of him started to fill my mouth. I like the way Meijo came. Not like a hose or a faucet, but in waves, like a woman, letting me take it in, and feel the warmth in my mouth and throat. He tasted so good and i wondered if you liked someone's taste because you liked them, or that liking someone's smell and taste was something that had to happen for you to fall for them.

He slowed down and eased back into the chair. I dropped my hands and kept my mouth where it was. I loved feeling him get soft again in my mouth while he pet my head. I waited patiently.

"I don't know if it's going to happen." Meijo whispered.

I stayed where I was. I also loved the feeling of him trying for me. Some day he would be getting soft like this inside my pussy.

And it would be amazing.

Finally, I could feel it. Just a slight warmth. He started and stopped. I caught it all in my mouth. I reached up and smacked his belly, pushing down.

"All right," He laughed. Then he let go. I could feel his piss pour into my mouth in a long stream.

I tried to let it pass right down into my throat but choked a little. He tried to pull back but I grabbed his ass again and secured my face onto his cock. He kept pissing and i drank all of it. It began to slow and I stayed there, waiting. He spoke.

"Oh, fuck that was so good."

I kneeled up. "Do you ever get upset that I still insist on being a virgin?"

"I get mad when you call me your little buddy."

I laughed. "Did I do that?"

"Do you want me to be your boyfriend?"

"I do. Some days, I think that's what I want. Other days, I don't know anything. And it's not you. It's something in my head." I pushed his legs up and started fingering his ass.

"If you think you aren't perfect…" he started. I knew how this was about to go. I bent back down and put my tongue in his ass. I pushed as hard as I could, tonguefucking him. I pushed the chair back and it laid out flat like a bed behind him. This was a 40,000 dollar chair called a KOZO that could basically adapt to any position. It was one of my favorite purchases. I pushed him up all the way onto it and spread his legs wider to get as far into it as I could.

"You could just say you don't want to talk about it." He began to moan again.

"I don't want to talk about it." I stood up and went into the other room. Here's something I know about men. If you put their legs in the air and play with their ass and then leave for a minute. You can tell just what they want you to do by what pose they are in when you return.

I pulled off my pants and shirt. I looked at myself in the mirror. What I see when I do that is kind of a secret. If you're nice to me, I may tell you later.

But for now, I pulled out the aerostrap and let it fall around my waist and lock. This was a pricey strap on with a configurable dildo.

The cock was set by default to be a little bigger than Meijo's. Here is the rule. Always fuck a guy with a cock just a little bigger than their own.

Make sure they know.

Back in the den, Meijo was in the same pose I left him. He was holding onto his cock as it lay limp between his legs. I moved over him laying there and straddled his face, facing his head.

"Can you lube me up?"

He nodded. I remembered the feel of his hands in my hair and grabbed his hair hard. It was nearly shoulder length now, smooth, black. I dug my fingers into it and used it to pull his face onto the cock. I knew the best lube was deep at the back of his throat so i pushed harder until I could hear him choking. I pushed down, trying to get into the deep back of his throat. It felt soft back there, velvety.

I pushed it in and out for a few minutes until it was glistening and I could see his spit dripping. I pulled it out and walked my way down his body until I was straddling the KOZO and in position to aim my cock into his open ass.

I looked at Meijo and put my fingers in his mouth. He started sucking them down as I pressed the dick into his asshole. My fingers were wet and hard in his throat and I could feel the opening in the back of his throat. Meijo laid there silent, impaled from both sides. I imagined I could get my hand so far inside I could touch the cock riding up his asshole. I pulled them both in and out in a rhythm.

"Are you going to do this thing with me?" I whispered at him.

He nodded and grunted while I fucked harder. I fucked his face and ass in unison, slapping his face.

"Open your eyes." I barked at him.

"Yes." he tried to say. It didn't work. I pumped harder. "Are you going with me?"

His eyes were wide as he nodded. His eyes were watering now as my fist violated his throat. But he couldn't seem to stop nodding and trying to say "yes" to me.

"Yes." he said with his eyes. I fucked him into the KOZO again and again. There was no more resistance in either his wide open mouth or his ruined asshole. Both were like caves I could explore. Both were mine. I felt my back muscles as I gave the last few strokes, thinking about the day when it was me on the KOZO.

Me opened up.

***

Meijo laid next to me, about half the way to sleep.

"So, you're going to do it?"

"Yes, and so are you. You agreed while I was tapping your ass."

"I like the body you're in."

"Well, maybe I just need to test drive."

"I'll come with you," he said as he drifted off to sleep. "But I don't want one."

I looked down at his perfect little body lying next to me. He might never really understand any of this.

And the next day, we went to LifeQuest.

Luna

Ok, so I should back up a little, maybe. I always feel like I have to explain why the year 2500 (Almost. Like, I say, we're only nine months away) doesn't really look all that different from the year 2000.

It's because of an orange cat.

I know, you're thinking that's just nuts, but, again, this is my journal and you're just a figment of my imagination so who cares what you think. This is my history lesson for today, figgy.

Set your internal clock to the year 2030. A few years earlier, in the United States of America, they elected a president, Stuart T. Essary, who was determined to tear everything down. He was basically anointed by a series of billionaires who wanted no rules for the hyperwealthy. That usually means many many rules for everyone else.

And it did this time, too.

The difference between the very wealthy and very poor grew greater and greater. Wars broke out. The government of billionaires blamed everything on a hyper liberal "shadow government" that was apparently at fault and was sabotaging all of their great results. At one point, the government declared martial law on the defenders of the shadow government.

Which was everyone they didn't like.

And they broadcast the skirmishes, showing everyone the heroes of the state, rounding up the bad guys.

In the midst of it, Stuart T. Essary, the president of the US, well, his likability ratings were going down, down, down.

It looked like he would be voted out by a progressive government.

Until May 17th.

On that day, the President's secondary residence, in the old state of Florida, was blown up. The press were there filming. And what they saw was Essary pulling himself from the wreckage heroically. And then, moments later, diving back in, only to re-emerge holding his own maid's orange tabby cat. The cat was alive and unharmed.

At that point, he could do no wrong. Everybody loved him. No one said a word when he doubled down on martial law. Or when he blamed the bombing on the shadow government. Or when he accused Canada and Mexico of participating, too, and annexed them, changing the name of "the United states of America" to the "Federated Republic of Essary," or "FRE," a giant, unwieldy conglomeration of entities that collapsed within four months, completely tanking the world economy and bringing nearly every other country on earth down with it.

What followed is considered to be the second dark ages. Power reverted back to the individual local governments, in some cases, back to towns, all of which made their own rules, laws, and mistakes. A lot of technology was lost. A lot of people died. Hell, they burned some more witches. It took hundreds of years to build back up.

Eventually, some semblance of the United States emerged again, what we live in today, seventeen loosely connected states along the west coast including the state of Baja, where I live.

Baja has been doing fairly well for the last 100 years or so, and is the home base of the more progressive United States Government that is on the rise, the Neonaughts, who wrested power in the last few elections from the Fedistes, a more conservative populist group.

The impact of the conservative groups was still heavy in the air, though. Masculine, traditionalist, etc.

It's also the home of Lifequest, a large biology company that I had never personally heard of until about a month ago, when they started advertising their Secondbody program, that, they claimed, could put your mind in a sexy loaner body for two days for only 10,000 dollars.

***

"Is this a good idea?" Miejo looked at me. I was still looking at the building.

"No." I took a deep breath. "It's a fucking amazing idea."

Rik pulled up next to us on top of the monocab. He stepped down and it scurried away like an urban cockroach. If you'ver ever felt that looking at one of those fuckers, you aren't alone.

"What did I miss?"

"Nothing." Meijo was unimpressed. I don't know how. I had been collecting the flyers for LfeQuest for the last month fantasizing about this moment.

Rik hadn't read any of them. "So what happens to your body when you walk out of here in some stranger's body?"

Meijo turned to me and crossed his arms, "Good question."

"Ok, first of all, it's not anyone's body. They grow them without a mind. You just step into it and then step out." I was now reciting the flyer.

"That is fucked up," Rik nodded.

"And we just leave your body with them?" Meijo was not having it.

I sighed. "Think of it like a test drive. I take the body, I leave my own."

"So your entire body is just collateral." I know Meijo was trying to make it sound awful, but it was just that simple.

"Like at a pawn shop?" Rik had never seen a pawn shop. There hadn't been one of those around for about a hundred years.

"Yes. My body is like the pawned item of property at a pawn shop and the new body is like a ticket." Nope, it still sounded stupid.

"Let's go in and get that ticket."

We walked up the steps into the big foyer area. This entry area was even bigger than I thought it would be, and reminded me of a museum. There were sculptures and paintings everywhere, depicting perfect chiseled bodies. I was keenly aware that they all looked more like Rik than either myself or Meijo. In the middle of it was a long desk with a flawless looking blonde woman sitting there typing. We watched her as we stepped toward the desk.

Now, two things.

They probably hired her to further this idea that this was a building full of perfect bodies for hire. Either that or they built her in the lab, One way or the other, well fucking done because she was basically the girl who would be in the photo in a book about beauty in the section on pure genetic perfection. There was literally nothing wrong with her. That was one crazy affectation.

Two, she was typing a lot. I'm fairly sure that the fairy tale hot receptionist in this building didn't have a novel's worth of work to do while checking people in for the Lifequest Secondbody program.

She was doing this, likely, to avoid the awkwardness of sitting there staring at us while we walked the nearly hundred yard span from the doorway to the desk area. Nothing she was typing was probably of any value.

She looked up at us and smiled. "Can I help you?"

Hi, I'm Sherry Osman and I have a noon appointment."

She looked at Rik and Meijo and then back to me.

"Oh, my bodyguards." I offered quickly

She checked her books and smiled, pointing to a red line on the floor. "Just follow that line up to the third floor, Ms. Osman." And handed me a badge.

So, now, I should explain who Sherry Osman is. She's a nobody, a cipher, she don't exist. My name is Seka Ogurd.

And, before you ask, yes, I was named for that Seka. The skater.

In 2458, there was this famous laserskater named Seka Kaska who lit up the Artsport world. Laser skating is a well respected artsport where you skate on a patch of ice beautifully with tiny lasers in your booties until you turn the ice into water, whereupon, you make your way through the watery ice, the icy water, and finally just water. It's a beautiful artsport. Kills lots of people every year.

At any rate, Seka Kaska was revered and had been doing this artsport and surviving for almost 30 years. People said she had impossible poise, eternal grace, and insane balance. During an interview, she once stayed balanced on the tip of one foot for the full one hour interview. No charlie horse. It was crazy.

My dad was crazy about her and named me after her. Which was great, as a kid. Everyone knew who she was, and there were a few Sekas in my generation. When I was 10, though, she was vacationing on an island and broke every bone in her body in a glider accident.

The accident left her permanently paralyzed from the neck down. In order to retrieve her and save her from this remote location, doctors onsite amputated her body and froze her head. They bright her back home and the doctors there were like, "What the fuck, island doctors?"

Apparently, to them, curing paralysis was something they were well on the way to doing. Curing head-no-body, though, was pretty far in the future. Head-no-body was a big problem and there was no almost-through-human-trials experimental drug that was going to fix that.

So with everyone in the world watching, doctors sort of packed her away apologetically, no way to thaw her out and no way to cure the other thing.

So, when I was 21, rather than live my public life in an episode of a "remember that incredibly famous public persona who had an awkward ending" trivia show, Meijo and I spent tens of thousands of dollars to get some new identities made. I was Sherry Osman, but also Sylvi Opperman and Sinka Ooze. That last one just made me laugh. Her middle name is "inda." Say it out loud.

Meijo had id as his real self, Meijo Lauda, but also as Mek Lorrado, famous spy, Mondo Lucha, world renowned wrestler, and Mocha Latte, extreme homosexual. That last one was my gift.

Rik was just Rik Ojimbiro. And he hated it when you mispronounced his last name. "Get some learning," he would tell you. And he's a big guy, so you would do that, you would go get learning.

We followed the red line to a massive elevator. Why would a place like this that had such a pricey service that only a rarefied community could purchase need massive elevators? To intimidate people. This entire place was built to do that. And, again, I'm 5'4", so I'm intimidated easily. I often think that it's possible I have a lot of meat on my bones because I'm fairly low on the food chain.

Which is also maybe a little hot. I don't know.

The elevator door opened on the third floor and we continued to follow the red line to a beautiful waiting room. I had expected something medical and antiseptic looking, white and clean. Instead this room looked like the foyer to an old luxury high end bordello. The walls were matte black, textured with tiny, beautiful pinstripes. There were green plants and flowers that looked like eruptions of red and orange all over.

The lighting was all coming from what looked to be a glass roof.

Decadent, overstuffed sectionals and massive ottomans in deep black and green gave the room a cozy feeling. It looked like a place you might throw a very high end sex party. There was an area covered in mirrors, where you could see yourself, ostensibly, from all sides.

There was a wall that was seemingly active, playing visuals of what looked like a swimsuit competition, threatening to become more lurid.

And on the other side of the room, a ruddy man in a white coat stood by a door.

"Hello, I'm Bron. This is the Launch area for you. That outside door is locked and you and your friends will have the only access to this area for the next two days. Everything you might need is here in the launch area. Behind this door here we will perform the procedure. It's very quick and should only take about twenty minutes. After that, you are on your own and you are free to stay here or go where you like. We just expect you back in 48 hours."

Bron was tall with taut, reddish skin. He was sort of ruggedly handsome. He didn't seem like someone who would be handing out pad tablets to people going through medical procedures in brothels, yet "here we are," I thought, as he handed me a pad tablet to sign.

I signed it and handed it back to him, following him out the door to the area behind.

Now, this was exactly as I had pictured. A white area with a circular hallway and a dedicated room in the center, with a long reclining table. It reminded me a bit of the KOZO at home and, for a second, I started to wonder why this service wasn't even more expensive.

Bron showed me a picture of the body I had chosen. It was designated "LUNA" and of all the bodies they had, it looked the most like me. But me, if I had been unbearably beautiful, 5'7" 132 pounds, with long dark hair, naturally smoky eyes and rich pouty lips. Her skin was nearly the same shade of olive as mine and they had tattooed her arms beautifully, in full sleeves that just made her look so much cooler. Her face looked kind, and innocent in a way.

Her eyebrows were thick and luxurious, like mine, but where nine always seemed to dominate and control my face, hers seemed expressive, like a tool a face could use.

I smiled and handed back the picture.

"You've read through all the rules," He said as I got up on the table. I nodded.

"Do I need to take my clothes off?" I looked up at him.

Hea leaned in, "Do you want to?" I admit that this was not un-creepy. I shook my head and filed it away for later.

I leaned back and breathed in slowly as Bron put wires and electrodes on my head. Once done, he sat down. "Ok, I just need you now to count down from 10 to zero."

I closed my eyes and squeezed my hands into a fist. "Is this going to hurt?"

He laughed, "Nope. You won't even feel it. Now, starting at 10..."

I started counting down. The room seemed to be spinning a bit so I closed my eyes even tighter. I started to relax a little as I got to five. And by the time I reached three, I could hear a change in my voice.

"And one..." I opened my eyes. My voice sounded different. It was more musical. It seemed to be in the same range, but somehow just more melodic. "Is my voice different?" I looked up.

Bron walked around the circular hallway and started to disconnect the wires from my head. I made a motion to sit up and snapped to a seated position as if on a spring. I swung my legs over the side easily. I felt like gravity had no effect on me.

"Whoa," Bron was there. He stopped me from falling over. "You need to get used to this."

I was in the Luna body.

I stood up.

I felt strong and bouncy. I felt like I could jump over his head if I needed to.

I padded over to the wall, where there was a full length mirror and saw luna. The first thing I noticed was that she was hunched over a bit. So, I fixed that.

I stood up straight. Her eyes really did look like mine. And when I smiled, her smile was similar, but where mine stopped, hers just kept going, until her entire face was open, wide, smiling. Her lips were perfect. She was wearing a thin black bra and black boyshorts with no shoes. I put my hands on the body's waist and could feel the taught, young skin—flawless.

I ran my hands over the curves. The difference between the waist and the hips were so pronounced. The body had a pierced bellybutton and the cutest, tiny indentation where it dipped into it, like a tiny little hill that kids might sled on.

Bron was watching me touch and become acclimated to the body. He was clearly turned on by it.

"So what do you think?"

"It's a beautiful body. It's amazing."

I looked around the room. I could see now that the patient area was on a dias in the center of the hallway. It had rotated around during the procedure and my body was now behind that wall.

"Is my body there?" I pointed.

Bron nodded. How many times had he been through this?

"It is, do you want to see it?"

I shook my head and followed him around the hallway to the other side. Walking was so easy now. I considered how long this body might be able to just walk and walk.

The other side was darker now and I felt a little twinge as I saw my body laying there. It didn't look asleep. It looked dead.

The face was drawn and empty and the mouth was slightly open. Part of me panicked, wondering how safe this all was. I realize, in retrospect, that this was a terrible time to begin to consider the safety of the procedure, but it all just started to wash over me.

"It's all good. This is exactly what is supposed to be happening."

"Does everyone do that the first time? Freak out about their body?"

"Absolutely, This is a weird thing, no doubt."

"And my body just stays here for 2 days?"

"It's being artificially fed and taken care of." He pointed to a tube going in my arm I didn't remember having been put there. "And this area is secure. Every transition room has its own launch area and they are only used by one client until that client's trip is over."

"So anything I leave here will be fine until I get back?"

He laughed again. His laugh wasn't bad. It wasn't one of those condescending laughs. It was really one of those laughs like people make when kids play with puppies for the first time. He seemed to be enjoying the newness of this for me.

"We can watch out for your purse, your body, your coat, anything you leave."

"And the guys I came with?"

"Right behind that door. The launch space is for you guys to use any way you want. And you can leave anytime. But. 48 hours. Be back."

"Got it." I walked toward the door and waved at him.

Pushing open the door, I saw Meijo and Rik lounging, waiting for me. They looked up when I walked in. There was a look of confusion on their faces. I wasn't sure what they expected when I came out after the procedure.

I stood up straight and put my hands in the air like a belly dancer, leaning my hips to one side.

"Hey, guys. Who wants to fuck this thing?"

Listen

"Wow. It really kind of looks like you." Meijo was still looking at the body like it was an alien or something.

"I know. It's so bizarre." I stood in the mirrored area and looked at it from all sides. It still looked round and curvy but the definition was amazing. It had a six-pack.

I pulled the boyshorts down to my knees and stared. The body was shaved completely. I spread my legs and I saw the body do the same in the mirror. Its pussy was compact, little, with tiny hidden away parts reaching down below. The lips were a bit darker than the olive skin around it. And if I pulled it open, it looked impossibly pink.

"Come look at this, guys. It's so cool."

"How do you feel?" Rik asked as he walked over. I raised my arms and he took the hint and took off the bra.

"I feel light, but kind of strong. I feel very awake. Like I have a lot of energy." I motioned Meijo to come over. "Here, put your fingers in here," I spread my pussy for him.

"Are you sure? I've never put my fingers in you before." he put his hands on the body's waist.

"I know. But it's like, in this body, anything goes, you know? Like i feel I can do anything." I took his hand and slid his fingers in my pussy. They felt so good.

"It's very wet." Meijo started moving around and I leaned back into Rik. I reached back and pulled Rik's fingers into my asshole. Leaning into him, I wrapped my arms around his neck. This was worth the 10,000 all on its own. I felt their hands in me at the same time and it seemed impossible to me that I could have had the hangups I did. Why wasn't I doing this every single day in my own body?

"Can you feel this?" Meijo had found the body's little spot and was moving his hand in the pussy at a steady rate now, hitting it on the upstroke. Rik's fingers were like liquid, moving in my ass at the same time. It felt stronger than it had in the past when I played with my own pussy.

"It's so nice and open." Rik's voice from behind me made me want to spread even wider and open my ass for him. He slid his hand in a little deeper and this body felt like some kind of sleeve connecting both men, letting them in as far as they could go.

Meijo hit a rhythm with his hand and I breathed out and let that happen. He placed one hand on the body's belly and pressed down a little so that the connection was perfect. My breathing began to conform to his movements, one breath in slowly for 4 piston-like movements, one breath out slowly for the next 4. I could even hear the cycle, the system of it, as the body fell into a familiar haze. I could tell this body had experienced double penetration before.

I heard the liquid sounds from between the body's legs as it started to cum, to squirt from the internal manipulation. It started as just an increased wetness but then grew to a stream, pouring from Luna's cunt while the belly seized up over and over. Rik jammed his hand in farther and I could feel her asshole brushing against his knuckles. Meijo kept moving, kneeling and trying to catch the liquid in his mouth while Rik began pushing upward with his arm, taking some of the weight off my legs. I tried to bear down on his fist while I was cumming.

Or was Luna cumming?

I closed my eyes and just heard the two men breathing. Rik put his hand around my throat to steady me and I pushed down harder on his fist, letting my legs lift off the ground. Meijo spread the body's legs wider and kept at it, sucking me and fingering me inside, I felt light, like I might float away. I wasn't even heavy enough to push downward on Rik's hand to pull his full fist into my open ass. I had one hand on Meijo's hair and one wrapped around Rik from behind.

Rik squeezed on my throat and that helped ground me a lot. It also gave me something to push against. I lifted my legs from the floor and put my feet up on Meijo's shoulders. The bottoms of the body's feet were impossibly smooth, as though she were a newborn. I pressed down, pushing the bottom of Luna's ass hard on Rik's fist until I felt a pop and his full fist was in its ass.

I could tell that this wasn't the first time that the Luna body had been fisted and I breathed in and out quickly, letting it settle on his fat hand while I was also supported by his other hand on my neck and my feet on Meijo's shoulders.

I started moaning in Luna's melodic voice and sprayed cum in Meijo's face again, hearing the sounds of him scrambling to catch and drink it all. He alternated between playing with Luna's clit and inner spot and I realized that this body was able to cum over and over alternating back and forth between internal and external orgasms. I was twitching and I felt out of control. But I felt light and airy enough to know that people could catch me, save me, take me.

I tried to think about the way my ass was invaded by Rik's massive hand. I imagined myself impaled on some ancient warrior, unable to free myself, while my other hole was used and taken advantage of.

I suddenly wished I had something in my mouth and felt greedy, like some kind of pig who couldn't get enough and never wanted it to stop.

Meijo's lips grabbed on to Luna's clit while his fingers played inside, riding back and forth against the g-spot.

He opened his hand a little and I could feel Luna's vagina stretching wider to accommodate his strong hand. I could feel something bigger welling up inside and I got closer to it every time I thought about the reality of the dual invasion of this body.

My body.

That was it. That was the thing that made it happen. As soon as I began to accept that this body was me right now, that it was me being invaded, being impaled, used, opened up, something unlocked. I started to moan in Luna's melodic voice, building to something.

"Oh, guys, fuck. I'm sorry. I'm cumming. It's so hard. It's so. I can't."

Suddenly, there was an explosion from inside and I let out a long moan while the body shook and for a second, I lost control of it. I slid to the floor, off of Rik's hand, down onto my knees. I put my head down on the warm black carpet and lifted my ass in the air.

The body was still cumming, still twitching.

"Are you ok?" Meijo was petting my hair. I burrowed into him.

"Yep. One second. I was still breathing really hard.

"Pretty wide open ass for such a tiny thing." Rik sat on the floor next to us. "Was that you or the body?"

"I don't know. Both, maybe. I've gotten some big buttplugs in, but I feel like this body is familiar with fisting. I think it can take a lot." I rolled over on my back and spread my legs. "Do you guys want to piss on me?"

Meijo got up on his knees and straddled my head. Rik stood up and pushed my legs apart. I lifted them up and realized how incredibly flexible this body was. I pulled my legs back so that Luna's pussy was totally exposed.

Meijo was semi-erect so he used his right hand to bend his dick downward. He leaned forward, trying to piss. I felt the warmth of Rik's piss stream on my open pussy and it felt so good.

I moved around and imagined catching all of it in my open cunt. The raw smell of piss circulated through the room and I licked at Meijo's dick, running my new tongue in and out of the little hole and tasting the brine of his pee.

I was feeling warm and used and it was topped off by the slow stream of urine that poured out of Meijo's dick onto my face. I licked at the stream and sucked it in. Everything still tasted the same with Luna's body, but things were more intense, stronger. I drank as much as he had in him and he rolled over, lying next to me. He took Luna's hand and closed his eyes.

"It's so weird. Your hand feels different. When you talk, I know it's you in there.

"Do you want me to shut up?" I laughed.

"Ha" Meijo responded. "The opposite." And then he kissed me.

We kissed a lot when I was in my own body. I didn't think much of it. But kissing in this body felt different. It felt less Like I was asking for something and more like I was giving something. I thought for a second about how badly my brain had been wired for so long.

I reached over and Kissed Rik. I was so grateful for him. He'd always been so easy going about me and my weirdnesses and kinks. From the beginning he was just good to me, playing or not. In his head, "Gay" meant "I like only guys, except for my friends, " and no matter what body i was in, he was just comfortable with me, the actual me.

I extended my arm and pulled Rik's pants down. He was partially hard. I ran my hand over his prick while I did the same for Meijo's lying next to me. Both of them got harder in my hands at the same time, which was an amazing feeling. I lifted my leg and straddled Meijo's body, shoving my ass in his face hard. I moved back and forth, massaging both of their cocks spitting on them and getting them wet.

I pressed down hard on Meijo's face, facing Rik, feeling the tongue pushing its way into Luna's ass. It was liberating. This ass was perfect.

It was something anyone would want to suck and lick. I felt so powerful wearing it, like I could do what I wanted with it. And people would say, "yes, ma'am," and take it.

Do some people feel like this all the time?

I lifted Meijo's cock and pulled Rik forward, sliding his dick into Meijo's open ass. I could feel him move under Luna's bottom now, pushing harder. Rik moaned and leaned over to kiss me.

I flipped around to talk to Meijo. Leaning in and kissing him, I felt that wonderful wet round mouth of his under me.

"I'm going to do this. Are you ready?"

He nodded at me and breathed in with every one of Rik's thrusts.

"I want you to close your eyes and pretend it's my real body. Is that ok?"

He smiled and nodded. I could tell he was already working not to cum. I climbed back over him and pressed Luna's pretty asshole in his face, kissing him with it. I was incredibly wet and I could feel it as I dragged this body's cunt over him, crawling toward Rik. I imagined I was leaving a trail down his body as I crawled, wiping this perfect pussy all over him.

I half stood as Rik pushed Meijo's legs up under me, leaving me free to slide down onto his cock. I faced Rik now and held onto My partner's pretty dick, placing the head of it right at the entrance to this beautiful cunt hole. I leaned forward and kissed Rik's chest as I descended onto Meijo's dick, sliding slowly down it while Rik kept a steady rhythm pushing into his ass.

As I locked into place, I felt like the three of us were connected now. I wrapped my arms around Rik and sucked on his nipples while I moved up and down on the cock buried deep in my hole. I tried to match their rhythm and felt my pussylips press down on his pelvis rhythmically with every thrust of Rik's dick into him.

I closed my eyes and imagined us as a complete system, a perfect chain.

I'd used dildos before, but it was so different feeling something alive inside me, the warmth, the movement. I could sense his prick breathing, pulsing, getting thicker even as it dripped inside me. Meijo's moans were plaintive and soft and tortured. I could feel how hard he was trying to make this time last, inside me.

I sucked at Rik's chest and let the body take over. I sank inside the blackness that was all around me with my eyes closed. My own cum was dripping down and I imagined it was lubricating Meijo's ass as Rik's thick stick violated him over and over. We increased the pace and I waited to feel, for the first time, what that eruption inside me would feel like. Was this body sensitive enough? Would I know it when Meijo came?

I wished that it were inside my own body. And realized that, in a way, I was jealous of this body I was in. I let myself fall into the black and opened my mind this time to Luna, looking for a spark, anything inside her mind that could tell me what she wanted.

But I found nothing.

Nothing but black.

Until, all of a sudden, there was. I saw it in front of me, floating in the black. It was Luna. Her body moved closer in the blackness. She spread her legs and I could see the perfect slit, wet and waiting, between them. The black swirled around me as it got closer. It was almost so close I could reach my tongue out and kiss it.

Until the lips moved and I could hear them say something, clear as day.

"Listen."

At that moment, Rik started moaning loudly. He grabbed at the body's tits and held on with one hand while his other hand wrapped around its throat. "I'm fucking cumming. I'm cumming."

His pace ramped up and the explosion happened under me. Meijo let out a long cry and it felt like everything underneath me had turned to liquid, warm and wet and thick.

My eyes shot open and the image of Luna dissolved. Meijo pumped a few more times and grabbed at me, digging his nails into the body's waist.

I rolled over, trying to figure out if This body had cum, too, but I realized it was impossible to tell. I laid on my belly and pulled myself over to the guys to clean off both their dicks with my mouth.

"That was fucking amazing." Rik laughed. He was right. I felt a twang of pain, thinking that we could have been having this kind of unrestrained fun all along except I had issues. I stood up and looked down at this body.

It was flawless.

It felt like this body could take so much more. I thought for a second about all my friends who would love to fuck this. It was a weird feeling, one I never had in my own body.

Meijo got up, "I am 100% sure they have booze here."

He wasn't wrong. It only took him a minute to find a couple of bottles of wine and one attractive bottle of champagne. I grabbed the champagne. This seemed like one of those situations where we all get our own bottle.

And I was celebrating.

Besides, cups were a little more elusive.

The thick black carpet felt soft and rich under me. I was keenly aware, though, that we were all dripping onto it.

"To carpet cleaning services," Meijo raised his bottle.

I opened the champagne and sat down crosslegged, taking a swig. "Fuck, yeah."

"I'm sure it's always a fucking swamp in here," Rik observed. He had a point. These rooms were probably abused on a daily basis. Good on them if they could keep them sanitized. In this new body, right now, though, I wasn't really worried about germs.

Was I now worried about anything?

I saw some of Meijo's cum in a small pool in between us. I put the bottle down and leaned down, licking it off the carpet. At that moment, I wished that many people had stepped right there in their boots. I wanted germs. I wanted the world.

"That was you." I looked over at him and he laughed. He could see how free I was feeling in this empty body.

But, was it really empty? I thought about the little hallucination I had had when I closed my eyes. When Luna appeared to me.

"Listen"

"What?" Rik looked at me and took a drink. He was sitting back naked propped up against a giant ottoman.

"It's what I saw the body say to me. In a vision. When I closed my eyes. Right before you pumped about a bucket of jizz up this guy."

"It was a lot. I feel like a water balloon." Meijo took a sip as well. He was drowsy, I could tell. Maybe we would crash here.

"Maybe it meant to listen to the body- to just let it take over?" Rik seemed interested.

"Probably." I stood up and walked around. It was strange how light I felt in this body. I explored the room. Here was a sort of half closet full of sex toys. Where was that 20 minutes ago?"

"Do you think it's something else?" Meijo sat up a bit.

"I don't know." I closed the door to the closet. On the front of it was a logo, It was a stylized "Q" that was the standard logo for lifequest. I squinted at it. I was thinking when I was collecting the flyers that it looked familiar to me. But I didn't know from where.

Now, a little tipsier, it hit me. I cocked my head and looked closer.

"Hey, guys. Is it possible that my trust fund is from LifeQuest?"

LifeQuest

The history of Lifequest is a bit of an up and down sort of roller coaster ride. Come along on this ride with me for a minute.

About 50 years ago, the company was founded by a man named Vero Kaine. Kaine based the whole thing on an invention he had.

Or maybe had.

You see, 2451 was the first year of the awakening. The whole world had been in the middle of a dark age for over 400 years. It was a brutal period of time. I had a friend who used to joke that it was the time in history where you could not get fancy cheese.

And that is kind of an understatement.

New governments were arising, trying to support learning and education and it was making a big difference for real. People were learning. Epidemics were going away, medical science was advancing once again. Education wasn't a bad word anymore.

People supported real knowledge again.

Now, drop into that, the Kunai Notebooks.

In what used to be the farthest area of Egypt, there is a country now named Kunai. Kunai was the site of a world history project in the year 2000, a project that took the bulk of human knowledge and stored it in a series of archival books and buried them in a time capsule set to open 450 years in the future. The hope was that mankind, so far advanced now that we looked down on our ancestors as little more than monkeys, would open these and see the paucity of knowledge they actually had to work with, and feel sorry for them, vowing never again to belittle their great-great-to-the-nth-power grandparents.

It didn't quite land that way.

Instead, the time capsule opened into a world where each of these notebooks was worth a fortune for the forgotten knowledge it had. Authorities all over the world tried to make sure that books weren't taken and utilized, stolen by individuals and companies to leverage the technology and science within.

But, money talks.

And so, in the middle of an oasis of ignorance and with no technological antecedent, Vero Kaine opened lifequest with a singular product offering. A revolutionary artificially intelligent sex robot with natural feeling skin and orifices that it called the "Erocite," a true sexual experience for the ages.

And LifeQuest was suddenly one of the largest and best funded companies on the planet.

And it wasn't that the Erocite units were that convincing. They really were not. It still felt potentially like fucking a toaster, some people said. But any port in a storm, other people said.

Because of the Senza Dolore.

That's probably where I should have started. For hundreds of years, during the dark times, the incel movement had grown. This was a movement of cisgender men who felt entitled to women and, when denied, put them down, demeaned, insulted, and hurt them.

The goal was to perpetuate patriarchal models of ownership.

As you can imagine, that went over badly with women. In fact, year after year, it went over less and less well. And despite the descent into darkness and impoverishment of education, the movement of women to eject men from their lives grew.

In one country it was called the 4b movement. In another, it was called "the hopeful." In parts of the US, it was called, simply, "W". But, near the end of the 2300s, all of them had merged into a single global movement called Senza Dolore or "Without pain." And the Senza Dolore were growing by the year.

There was a gender war. And LifeQuest had produced the primary weapon for men in that war, in the form of a warm little sex robot that never said no.

But that wasn't all LifeQuest had up its sleeve. 22 years later, in 2473, after a number of Erocite upgrades, LifeQuest released its second product. It was a tool designed to be used by the very wealthy, an expensive room-sized box that could be used to create a living, temporary, subservient woman for your own uses.

The device was called "the bubble," and it was composed of a vat of protoplasmic matter and a complex computer that would configure the matter to make up the kind of woman you wanted, one that would last for up to four days before dissolving back into its component parts.

Years later, there were rumblings that the Erocite program was discontinued. The robots would eventually fall in love, if treated well. And, in over 90% of cases, they fell in love with women or other robots, something their onboard reasoning systems considered most rational.

Later, news reports released stories of horrific abuses that were committed against the protomatter automatons produced by the bubble. People were concerned that use of the device was causing people to become cruel, willfully hurtful. That they were abusing the things that were birthed by the bubble.

So, years later, this product offering slowly faded from its inventory. LifeQuest became a company focused on small pieces of genetic based technologies that helped people live "better lives" as it said in its advertising. For many men, the unwritten promise was that these lives could be had without the annoyance and frustration of women.

Whenever possible. In small ways.

Until just recently, where a large and costly ad campaign began, promoting the idea of a SecondBody for everyone, a body where you could act out the fantasies that you had without anxiety.

Again, If you were very wealthy.

***

Back home, I went looking through my records. I knew I had seen the Lifequest logo on an official trust document, but I couldn't find it.

I tried to make myself remember. Truthfully, in this body, my memory seemed to be working a lot better.

"Are you going to be naked all the time now," Meijo slapped the body on the ass on his way by. We were having a little get together with friends and he was right. I couldn't force myself to put clothes on.

I walked into the den still carrying a load of papers. Rik's brother Eiko was there in the pit sitting next to him when I plopped down.

"I feel like it's in here somewhere." I placed the pages on the poly table. It was clear so you could see your feet. I don't know why, honestly.

It's so crazy. That is so real. And it's beautiful." Eiko was fascinated by the body.

"Do you want to feel?" He came over and sat by me, fondling the breasts.

"So you can feel this and everything?"

"Oh she feels it all," Rik laughed.

"Damn." He was staring everywhere. "Can you cum like this, in this body?"

"Oh, god, it cums over and over. Do you want to feel the pussy?"

He looked up at Rik. Rik shrugged. I swung over and sat in Eiko's lap. All this talk about the body while I was in it was keeping me constantly wet. It was the weirdest objectification kink ever. I reached down to pull out Eiko's dick and slide it up Luna's cunt. He grunted once.

"Wow. Are you sure this is okay?"

"Yeah. I can do whatever I want with it for 48 hours. Do you want to see how fast I can get you off?"

I wanted the whole room to chant and cheer me on. Maybe next time. One or two of our friends were very into it, though. I caught Meijo's eye and he walked over. He pulled his hand out of his pocket and slid his finger in my mouth.

I put my hands on the couch behind Eiko and started bouncing up and down rhythmically. I sucked on Meijo's finger as I did it. I pushed down hard on Eiko's thick dick, and enjoyed the depth of it. Every time I came down, my clit hit the curved place where he was bent, sitting up in the couch. It was perfectly aligned.

Meijo slid another finger in my mouth and I widened my mouth a little. This was the forth fuck I'd had since we got back home and I had been able to cum each time. This time, though, I felt like it could be big. Eiko was big with wide black shoulders and a cock that matched. I tried to slam the body's cunt down as hard as possible in his lap and each time I hit, the tingle from my clit was powerful and building.

I grabbed Meijo's hand and tried to push it all the way into my mouth. He took his other hand and started choking me. Now he looked like he was trying to fist fuck my mouth, jamming it in harder and harder.

I kept my hands on the back of the couch and tried to open my throat, letting his hand as far in as possible. I arched my back and hoped people could see the body working. In my head, I thought about how it felt to "give rides" to my friends on this remarkable contraption, this body that was like a finely tuned car. I felt someone stick a finger in my ass as i came down hard on Eiko's prick and I tried to tell them, whoever they were, "More."

I wanted more.

Was this who I was, naturally? I tried to feel if some advanced sort of hypersexual hormone cocktail was present, but in reality, it just felt like me. My peripheral vision closed in a little as the choking and fist fuck of my throat began to affect my oxygen supply. As the blackness started to descend, I heard a grunt and a huge noise from Eiko.

He poured what seemed like wave after wave of cum in my open pussy, while the person who had been fingering the body's ass held tight, feeling his dick through Luna's thin internal walls. I slowly kissed Rik's brother while the person massaged his cock through my ass.

"10,000 dollars?" Eiko looked at me, in between kisses.

"I know, right? Worth it."

I wondered why I never thought before to have a naked party. I looked around. Meijo had his pants off and our friend Emmi was playing with his cock while they talked. Emmi was thin with almost no breasts. She was Chinese and had an adorable, short cropped head of blonde hair. She had joked earlier about putting her combat boots on and kicking this body's cunt over and over. I laughed back, but I think she wanted to do it.

Across the room, two girls were topless, kissing. One of them, a pretty redhead, spit into the other one's mouth. I know what that feels like, to want that.

And Eiko was standing up, taking his shirt and pants completely off.

He looked free. How skin was dark, but patchy in places. He looked like he might have been burned on one arm. His dick hung low, soft now, but long, swinging between his legs. He wasn't that thin. He had a bit of a belly, and it rolled when he laughed. It was what had slammed into my clit so hard while I was bouncing up and down on his prick.

He wasn't beautiful, but he was beautiful, if you know what I mean.

I crawled over and grabbed Eiko's ass and spread it open, licking it, pushing him against the far wall. He started laughing but realized nearly instantly how much he liked it. I pressed my tongue into his asshole as far as i could. My mouth was warm and wet and I wanted it to feel like a warm bath for him, like something lazy and soft and easy. I got up and told him to wait right there.

I realized that this fantasy of having people cheer me on wasn't going away. It was real, and here, among my friends, I could do it.

I grabbed Emmi's boots and brought them over to her. Winking at Meijo, I put them on her. I led them over to where Eiko was still leaning up against the wall.

With Emmi behind me, I got down on all fours and spread my legs. I put my face up into Eiko's waiting ass and started to warm it again with Luna's tongue, which was long and thick and capable. I closed my eyes and waited and sucked hard on the ass in front of me. Eiko tasted pink and sweaty and good. I tried to fuck his little hole with my tongue while I braced myself for what was coming.

Then I felt it. Emmi's boot crashed into the body's sloppy wet cunt making a wet splashing sound. It hurt. It was a pain that ran up the stomach and into the chest.

And I heard everyone cheering and yelling "ONE"

I sucked harder, licking at Eiko with my new lips and tongue and hoping it felt as good to him as it did to me. And the second one hit.

"TWO"

The sound was amazing. You could actually tell how wet Luna's pussy was from the smack. And I could feel the liquid from this body's cunt run down the legs, on both inner thighs. I spread my legs wider and kept sucking.

"THREE"

This one was harder. The smack resonated across the room and I could hear people audibly wince. This pussy dripped onto the floor and I saw red rip across the inside of my eyelids. I sucked Rik's brother's ass and felt a tear come down. I wish that Emmi could see that she was making me cry.

"FOUR"

Her boot lifted Luna's ass into the air and made me unconsciously groan, grabbing onto Eicko. I held his dick as I dug my face deeper into his ass, crying and lickng.I tried not to squeeze too hard, just holding his cock and balls.

"FIVE"

The tip of the boot dug into the cunt, connecting to Luna's pelvic bone. I breathed heavily and felt myself sliding down Eicko's body. He pushed my head down on the floor and held my arms behind me while other people pulled the body's legs apart.

I tried to elevate Luna's ass as the legs were pulled outward.

The kicks came harder now, and faster

"SIX, SEVEN, EIGHT"

Three in rapid succession, I screamed and started crying. I tried to lift the body's ass even higher and keep the legs spread. It was completely red behind my eyelids now.

"NINE, TEN, ELEVEN"

Three more, aimed adroitly at the body's inner lips. Luna's clit was aching, begging for pain, for attention, for anything. I could feel liquid dripping out of my open cunt onto the floor. People were laughing and cheering.

"TWELVE, THIRTEEN, FOURTEEN, FIFTEEN."

They came so fast, in a row, that I couldn't breathe. I let go and started bawling. "Please, please, please," I begged Emmi to wreck my cunt and destroy me. For a moment, I was afraid she'd stopped. "Twenty, Twenty, please."

Everyone cheered. I felt a hand between my legs. It was Meijo. "It's so fucking warm. It's on fire."

I realized that I was completely on fire. I was alive. I begged.

"SIXTEEN, SEVENTEEN, EIGHTEEN, NINETEEN, TWENTY."

Everyone cheered. I was sobbing. The body felt so raw and drained, but it was alive. It was powerful. It could take anything. I rolled over and felt between luna's legs. There was some blood. But mostly it was cum, and the slick wet of this body's pussy. Emmi put her boot near my face to show me the blood that was there. With my left hand I pulled the boot toward me and licked the blood from it. With my right I played with Luna's clit, massaging it franticly. I was so close. This body was so close.

Luna and I came together, on the floor, in front of everyone, with Emmi's boot in my mouth. I closed my eyes and breathed in.

When I opened them again, I could see the papers i'd strewn across the table. Meijo brought me a drink.

"Are you allowed to get that thing bruised up?" He handed it to me.

"I think I'm not getting my security deposit back." I drank.

Emmi sat down and put her hand on my belly. She kissed both eyes, licking at my tears. "Oh, my god, that was hot. This body can take a ton of abuse." I held her hand and leaned in to kiss her. She kissed me back with a warm open mouth.

"I cried so hard."

"I know. I loved it." Her top was starting to fall now, and I could see her right nipple, almost flush to her chest. I wanted to play with her flat chest but I had the sense that she would push me away. "Anything but that," she would think.

"Are you ok?" Meijo put his hand on the body's belly. I remembered hating that. But I leaned back and enjoyed it.

"I am. And check this out." I leaned over and grabbed a page from the mass on the transparent table. The one I'd seen from the floor through the table.

It was a picture of me as a kid, with an older man, in front of a bunch of papers and diplomas. I showed Meijo.

"Who is that?" He took the paper.

"That is Djinn Maretti, my accountant. And that is his office, with a ton of papers on the wall. Including that one. I pointed.

It was the lifequest logo. Slightly obscured. But there was no doubt.

Emmi looked over. "Yup," She nodded at Meijo, "You know that guy, too."

"I do."

"Yeah,:" she continued. "He's the settlement guy. He manages a bunch of trust funds for people. My dad knows him. you know. 'when your life has gone a bust, let Djinn Marreti do your trust '"

"And how would I know him?"

"Besides the catchy jingle?" she looked at us. "There's a billboard for his office like a block from your place."

Meijo looked at me. "Hm."

"Dude, we should do that again in your real body, if you can handle it." Emmi got up and downed her drink.

I put my hand between the body's legs. Could I handle that? With my actual pussy?

I think I could. I smiled at her. Then I looked over at Meijo.

"Hey. you don't happen to remember where you live, do you?"

Djinn Maretti

Being in my own body again felt heavy, oafish, in a way. I felt ungraceful, a victim of gravity. I felt myself hunching over and tried to stand up straighter.

"It looks like you enjoyed yourself." Bron winked at me. He was a confusing person. He was surrounded by half naked beautiful bodies all day long. Why did I feel like he was only hitting on me when I was in my actual body?

"I did. I bruised it up a bit, didn't I?" I actually felt kind of bad about that. "Do I need to pay more? Am I in trouble?"

He made a motion with his hand and shook his head. "Nah, it's all good. Honestly, I've seen way worse. Trust me."

The way he said that made me cringe a little. And then, unexpectedly, feel a sudden need to protect Luna. How much worse?

"Hey, let me ask you a question. How much would it be to reserve that body, let's say, if I wanted to. Just so that no one else uses it? "

"Welp. I could look into that. Usually, you would need to pay the standing rate. I might be able to work something out." He moved in closer to me.

In my head, I ran this through my hotness filter. The fact that he was into me, even surrounded by all these bodies was not unhot.

I tried to appear flirty.

"What can you do?"

"Well, I can easily keep her marked as checked out until you want her. And that would cost you nothing."

Would it, really, though? This was interesting.

"I'm not going to fuck you. I mean, I appreciate it, but..."

"No, no, not that. Look, I see a lot of naked plastic sort of bodies. Why don't you show me a real, pretty girl natural human body."

"So, show you my body?"

"All of it."

Here was the fantasy filter I could use for this. I was sacrificing my modesty to preserve Luna's safety. All I had to do was to whore myself out a bit, expose myself to Bron, and she would be safe. This, too, was not unhot.

"Ok, if I do this, you keep Luna checked out until I come to use her?"

"Yes."

"You know how many people have ever seen me undressed?"

"No, I don't."

"Like maybe 3 people. Altogether."

He paused and looked at me to see if this was really going to happen. "Am I going to be 4?"

I stood up straight. I looked him in the eyes. Why was this so hard? I had done so much worse in the last 48 hours in Luna's body.

Now, in my own. Wow.

I pulled my shirt over my head.

It was black and stretchy and it defined my boobs fairly nicely. I folded it in front of me and placed it on the table.

Kicking off my shoes I unbuttoned my pants and rolled them down. I folded them up and put them with my shirt. My clothing was all very light, and I was not expecting to be doing this in front of someone today. I reached between my breasts and clicked the clasp, causing the straps on my bra to retract and the enclosure to open, I slid it off and placed it on the table.

I took a deep breath. Bron was smiling at me. I let my hands fall and he stared at my exposed breasts. This was so much harder than anything I'd done in the last forty-eight hours.

"All of it." he pointed toward my underwear. I reached down and pulled them down, stepping out of them while leaning against the table. I folded them and placed them on top of the rest of my clothing.

"Nice. Natural" He walked around me, looking. "What's your favorite part of your body?"

I thought for a second. I was actually beginning to get wet. It occurred to me that I'd like him to see that. That if he saw anything, he should see that.

"My pussy, probably." I looked at him and he smiled.

"Can you show me? Show me and we're done."

I leaned back against the table and spread my legs. With one hand I opened up my pussy and showed him. He took a deep breath and paused, looking at me.

"Ok. I'll keep her checked out until you need her."

He turned and walked around the circular corridor.

I grabbed my clothes and returned to the Launch room.

In there, Meijo and Emmi were laughing and drinking wine from the remaining bottles. They came up and hugged me.

"Why are you naked?" Meijo whispered to me, worried.

I leaned in to him, "I'll tell you later."

Emmi looked at me, "ok, before you put them back on. Three kicks."

I did want to know, honestly, if I could take it as well as the Luna body did. But I also wanted something else. "You can do five. If I can have one thing."

Emmi came in closer and kissed me. "What do you want?"

I took a deep breath. "After, if I can take five, you let me suck on your nipples for five minutes."

Her smile dropped as she looked a little panicked. She started to pull away.

"You don't have to if you don't want to. But I really want to. And one other little thing," I whispered in her ear.

She was still wearing combat boots and a little plaid skirt. Her shirt was black now, though, and it hung off of her. I pulled her to me, "maybe I can't even take five. But I want to. Don't you?"

She smiled and nodded.

Meijo took my clothes and tossed them on the ottoman. I felt more naked than I ever had. I slid down to the floor and got on my hands and knees, spreading my legs. Meijo got on the floor and Held my legs open. I pulled away automatically when his hand went near my pussy.

And he noticed.

What was wrong with me?

I grabbed onto him and kissed him hard. He sank into me and held my head in his arms, petting my hair.

Emmi stood over me. I lifted my ass into the air. The first kick landed hard, directly in the middle of my cunt. It was like an electric shock.

But, surprisingly, it hurt less than it had when I was in Luna's body.

"Again," I called out. Her boot came down again, this time hitting my clit directly. A wave washed across me and I inhaled sharply.

"Harder." I could hear her step back and put herself into it. The flat of her boot's top hit my cunt perfectly, making that wet smacking noise it had made last night.

I breathed in. "harder" I moaned, although I wasn't so sure I meant it. This time, I felt the boot laces from the top of her shoe as they slammed their way up inside my cunt. My eyes started to water and I hugged Meijo tighter.

"C'mon, you fucking bitch. Break my cunt. Do it." I held on tightly to Meiijo for this last one, as she slammed her boot with incredible force, digging the top deep into my pussy, with enough impact to shake every bone in my body. For a second, I saw black and a wave of fire raced across my whole body. I felt like I had been fucked with her foot.

"Are you ok?" Emmi kneeled down by me. I could feel my submission kicking in, making me want to caress and kiss her boot. I wrapped my arm around her tiny waist and breathed heavily, tears coming down my face. I pressed my face up against her chest like an animal and she leaned back on one arm, lifting her shirt. I could see her skirt fall backward and could see her shaved pussy under it. She was wet, too. I pushed her down and sucked at her nipples like some kind of rutting piglet trying to feed on her. My cunt hurt impossibly badly, but it felt so good to be doing this in my own body.

I licked at her nipples and sucked them hard. I could tell she felt awkward about her chest and I didn't care. That was rude of me, maybe, but her completely flat chest was turning me on at that moment. The idea that she shied away from it, the way I shied away from my belly made me want to suck it and lick it.

Meijo kept petting my head and rocking me and It felt like more than 5 minutes.

But it wasn't enough. I wanted to tell her how much I loved her chest as she put her shirt back on.

But what was I? I wasn't exactly the paragon of body positivity, too scared to do half the things I did in another body in my own. Too freaked out to enjoy it when my own partner moves his hand toward me.

I sighed and put my own clothes on.

Yeah.

Who was I?

Rushing to spend 10,000 a pop to spend time in some strange body to do what I could do now if I wanted.

But still, as the three of us left the launch room, all I could think about was the Luna body, back there, in the dark, unused...

Waiting.

***

"Can you think of any reason why my memory might be better in one of those SecondBodies than in my own body?" I looked over at Emmi as we approached the billboard.

"I can't. I guess. Unless there was some organic physical cause? Like if you had some brain damage that was physically affecting your memory?"

I was trying not to think about the fact that she wasn't wearing underwear. That's my brain damage, I think. I know Meijo wanted to fuck her. That was hot, too.

Meijo pointed up. "There it is." The Billboard above us showed a thin man with a white lion's mane of hair. It said he was "Djinn Maretti, the Settlement king."

I looked up and then at Meijo. "Damn. I didn't know he was royalty."

Emmi stared at it. "I think this billboard has been here since the 70's. They just left it. Unchanged."

I hadn't seen him in a while, I confess. "Long live the king."

"So, he's like, 30 years older than that," Meijo pointed up at the billboard.

"He's a ghost."

Since the office was directly below the billboard, it didn't take us long to find it. But I wasn't expecting it to be just a computer driven warehouse.

We got the foyer and followed the signs, walking downward to an elevator that brought us even further downward. I imagined we must be at the 3rd or 4th sub basement,

The doors opened to a sign on the far wall that said "Djinn Maretti, Co." Under the sign was a terminal. For the first time in a while, as I said, I entered my own name and identifier. Under the name and Identifier number there were many other fields like "date" and "location." I left those blank.

It scanned my retinas and the door opened. We walked in and were suddenly aware of how big the world can be.

Three rows of files stretched down as far as the eye could see.

"Do you think there is a bus coming anytime soon?" Meijo asked.

I looked at him. I suppose we'd have to walk. Making it easy for us was that, about 400 feet down was a space that was lit up in a blue light. There was a holographic arrow pointing down to a file cabinet.

"Is this super high tech or super low tech?" Emmi wondered out loud.

I decided that someone must have thought this was the best way. And we moved toward the cabinet. It opened easily and I pulled out a file with my name on it.

It was that easy. The file was about one inch thick with papers. I opened it and saw a series of bank statements, financial models, etc. I looked through them and saw a start date. July 11th, 2487.

When the accident happened. It must be.

There were a bunch of other papers in there labeled "Work Product," but sure enough, on the first page was the Lifequest logo.

I had remembered it.

"Is that it? The logo," Emmi looked through the papers. I nodded.

"Hey, check it out." Meijo pointed to another arrow just about 100 feet further down. "Is that you, too?"

"Do you think I'm so cool, I have multiple files?"

"Probably," He yelled from 100 feet away.

Emmi and I walked over and looked at the cabinet. This one was a bit harder to open but after some struggle I got it to open. There was another file in there, again about an inch thick. This one said "Mika Spencer."

"That's not me." I wondered why it was illuminated.

Emmi grabbed it, "Maybe you have even more names than you thought, Mika Spencer."

"Am I a spy?" I started wondering. This could be cool. It was one of my favorite schizophrenia episodes. I'm a spy and everyone wants to kill or fuck me. They eventually decide just to fuck me.

"Look at that." She pointed to the inception of the file.

July 11th, 2487.

Meijo's gears were spinning, "Maybe you weren't alone in the accident."

"What happens if I take this file, too?" I looked around.

"Are you asking someone?" Meijo looked around, too.

Emmi ran her fingers over the cabinet. Dust. "How often do you think people come here?"

The two files had more in common than that. Under the name, on each one, was a stamp. It said "P-REF: LQ77"

I looked up at both of them. "Does that ring a bell at all? LQ77? And what is a P-REF?"

Meijo shook his head. Then he looked up. "P-Ref, huh? Hold on. Stay here."

He ran to the entry door. Opening it back up, he propped it fully open with a box sitting in the entryway. We saw him step up to the terminal and suddenly, all the lights dimmed.

"Ok, that's off. Are you trying to scare us?"

"Just wait for it." He started typing onto the terminal.

With a deep clicking sound, blue lights lit up the room. There were about a hundred holographic arrows up and down all the aisles.

"The room seems a lot more festive now"

I looked at Emmi. "And a lot more informative."

***

Emmi came back to my place with us and Rik was already there. I had asked him to set up his computers in the den near the kitchen so he could work here sometimes and he was just finishing. Rik was so quiet sometimes, but the keys clacking would let us know he was there. Like belling the cat.

We dropped handfuls of files Right near his workspace.

"Is this work for me?" he looked up.

I gave him a hug, "No, but there may be fun stuff in there."

"I see you are in your own body tonight?" Rik stepped around and flopped on the front couch in the pit.

"Actually, I brought a different body." I looked at Emmi and she nodded. Our other little thing.

I went into the drawer and pulled out the cloth tape. It was wide and soft and black. I grabbed Emmi by the shirt shock of blonde hair and pulled her to me, wrapping tape around her mouth so she couldn't speak. Meijo stepped back in surprise and slid into the overstuffed chair. I pulled off Emmi's shirt and wrapped it around her eyes, pulling tape over it around and round until she couldn't see at all. She tried to hold my hands as I dragged her by the hair and pulled her shoes off. "I thought this could be my pussy tonight." I yanked at her tiny skirt and it came off in two pieces, wrapping around her cute little ass as it pulled taught then off.

She tried to fight back So I pulled her hands behind her and wrapped the tape tightly around her belly, securing them as well. I slapped her flat chest until her nipples stuck out like thick fingertips, then taped each one down with a big black x.

Meijo was touching his cock watching, fascinated. Rik was amused himself, putting up one leg to observe.

I dragged her over to Rik and spread her legs. "This is my new pussy. You want to feel it?"

He put his fingers in and moved them around, "It's pretty good. It's tight enough."

"Do you want to see the ass?" I turned her around and spread her ass cheeks. He put a single finger in her and moved it back and forth. '

"Now that's even tighter." He laughed and spanked her hard.

I shifted over to Meijo. "Will you fuck my pussy, baby?"

"Of course, sweetheart. Do you want me to get off in you? Knock you up? It would be so nice."

I kissed him hard on the lips and pushed Emmi down on the ground on her back. I dropped down and knelt over her belly, spreading her legs and pulling Meijo down, too. I started massaging her clit. "I do, I want it. Can you come fuck it? I'm so wet for you."

Emmi's pussy WAS getting wet. In mock frustration, I slapped at her thighs, pushing her legs farther and farther apart. I leaned back and dropped my other hand onto her face, pushing her down. I know she couldn't speak or see, but she could feel that.

Meijo crawled over to us and pulled off his pants. "It's be nice to finally hold you and fuck your cunt."

"Yes, baby, I want it so bad." I kissed him really hard and pulled him close. I imagined that it really was me he was fucking as i pulled his cock into Emmi's hole. She squirmed under me and I slapped her over and over. "Is it good?"

"Oh, fuck, that's tight. It's beautiful. I'm so glad everyone left and I can just make love to you."

Rik laughed silently. I pulled Meijo closer and we got into a rhythm. I kissed him hard. "I'm glad that blonde bitch is gone and it's just you and me. Will you fuck me, baby? Harder?"

"I'll fuck you as hard as you want. I want to fucking breed you so bad. I want to put a baby in you."

"Oh, that would be so good." I yanked her legs open again and, behind me, slapped her face hard. Something happened and she went limp and stopped pushing back. I put my arm around Meijo and held on while, with the other hand, I played with Emmi's clit. The sounds coming from her cunt were getting wetter and wetter. Under my ass I could feel her tummy begin to spasm as though she were cumming.

"Oh, yeah, that's so wet." Meijo seemed to be loving it.

"That's right, baby. I'm always wet for you."

"I want to fuck your pretty asshole."

"Oh, yeah, Mei, fuck this ass." I pulled her legs up higher as he extricated his dick. Still holding her clit on one hand, I put my fingers in her cunt and yanked it upward, exposing that little pink asshole. He cock slid into it easily as she grunted under the tape.

"Get in my ass. C'mon, baby, wreck that fucking asshole."

"Yeah, I love this. I'm going to cum so hard up this fucking hole."

"Rip it up, baby. You know I love that pretty dick with no lube. Just shove it in." Meijo looked at me and I could tell he was about to cum.

"I love you, baby. I love you. Cum, please. Just let go in me."

I had never said that to him before and I knew the effect it would have. He moaned and pumped harder. "I love you, Se. So fucking hard."

"Then cum for me. Dig deep into that ass and use me."

He yelled out and started cumming. "Fuck." And we stayed like that for a little bit, with his cock getting soft inside Emmi. I knew she would remember this. I remembered that he said he loved me.

***

"So, you're both getting a body for tomorrow?" Rik was sitting at the computer trying to help us make the appointment. Sometimes he was like the concierge for all of us.

"Yep. Are you sure it's ok?" Emmi looked over at me. She was still naked, leaning against Meijo in the pit.

I was nice enough to remove the tape.

She still had redness where two black x marks adorned her chest. She had put her boots back on, which was crazy hot.

"Hell yeah, you were my co-spy today. It's not like I can't afford it."

"So what do I put her name down as, Sherri?"

"You do phony names?" Emmi sounded really turned on by the rulebreaking. Meijo had his fingers in her asshole and she kept pushing down on them. I loved that she was feeling good being topless.

"Yes. I mean, I'm paying out of a proxy account so any name you want to give is fine. "

"I can use a name from one of these files. One sec." Rik leaned over and opened one at Random.

"Hm." He opened another one. He typed a bit. "Weird."

"What's weird." I walked over to where Rik was.

"I put in Maya Greene, from this file. I put in her identifier and it kicked it back. No available reservations."

"Are they full?"

"No, look, I can book you with the Sherri Osman name and identifier. Now, this one, from this file, Sonal Okunde, with this identifier, aaaaaand...." he typed it in and there was a beep. "Same thing. No available reservations."

"How many did you try?"

"Six people from these files. All kick back. Laronna Michales, Tianna Seventeen, Melan Orande, and on and on."

Meijo called over, "Hey, are all those files women?"

I looked through them. Walking out to where Meijo and Emmi were sitting, I collapsed into the couch.

"Yes. They are. All women."

ZOESIS

Mika

Emmi and I left Meijo and Rik in the launch room while we talked to Bron before the procedure.

"Do you have two people at a time like this often?" I asked him while he was setting things up. Emmi was sitting on one of the two tables.

"Yeah, totally, Sometimes even married people. Boyfriend, girlfriends. You know, it's predominantly men who do this."

Emmi looked at me, "Really?"

"Yeah, like probably 90%"

"So, you remember our deal?"

"I do. And I've been keeping up on it. That's why you get me when you check in."

"We were wondering if you would want to, sort of..."

Emmi stood up. "Build on that deal."

"This is interesting. Ok. I'm listening."

I went on. "Would you say we are both normal, natural, but pretty girls?"

"I absolutely would."

We're trying to learn all about this. And we were wondering how trustworthy you are."

"I am very trustworthy. Absolutely."

I looked at Emmi. She started pulling her clothes off.

"The two of us will strip for you. You can look all you want at our bodies while they are here. You can even fondle. No inserting anything. And the panties stay on."

Emmi was naked now, down to her panties. She affirmed. "The panties stay one."

"Ok, I like it. I like it a lot. What do you want in exchange?"

I pointed to his portable computer.

"Oh. my computer."

"A loan. For a week. So we can learn about all this."

"Look, there's not much in there. I'm in the Zoetics group. It's the life maintenance group. My whole thing is just about these bodies and how to keep them alive."

"That's our deal."

"Well, yeah. I'm in. Hell, keep it. I'll report it broken and get a new one."

I started to get undressed and got up on the table.

"Just be kind, please."

***

I was in the Luna body when I stepped back into the Launch room, holding the computer in a small bag. And as hot as that body was, Emmi's choice was the really remarkable one.

She had chosen a male body named "Savi." It was 6 foot 2 Inches tall with dark olive skin, darker than mine. It was deeply muscled with short dark hair and what looked to be a permanent thin dark stubble. Both bodies were in black t-shirts and thin black pants today.

Rik looked up at Emmi. "Damn. That's what I'm talking about."

"Check this out," She unbuttoned the pants and pulled them down to right under the ballsack of the body. Out flopped a massive 12 inch dick that was so thick around I probably couldn't have gotten my hand around it. It was still soft, too.

Rik whistles. It was far bigger than him. "Will that thing even get hard?" He walked over and put it in his hand, feeling the weight of it. He started massaging it until, within a minute or two, it was pointed upward, at least an inch or two longer.

I was fascinated, "how does that feel?"

Emmi had her eyes closed. "I don't even know how to describe it. It's like getting turned on but more powerful and brutal. It's like being hungry. Like I couldn't stand it if he stopped."

Rik kept it up, "Do you want to fuck something?"

Emmi nodded. I looked over at Meijo. "Do you want to take it?"

"I don't know if I can."

"I never even pegged anyone. I'm not qualified to have this thing."

"We'll have a party tonight and you can use that thing on anything you want." I grabbed Meijo and kissed him with Luna's lips. "You want to just have a quickie with him before we go?"

I pointed with one hand at Meijo in my arms. "He fucked YOU last."

The Savi body was huge, and powerful. I wasn't sure I'd ever seen anyone fucked that hard. And Emmi was completely taken in by the urgency of that giant member, pulling it out and pushing it back in again and again, over and over.

Meijo went limp and Savi's face filled with a primal heat. The thick stick between Savi's legs was like a jackhammer, burrowing into Meijo's sweating ass.

Emmi, in the Savi body, groaned and sweat and moaned as the body lifted up over and over and pounded downward. She seemed to have lost all control.

Meijo started moaning and making these little sounds. I bent down and heard him.

"I'm sorry, I'm sorry. Just do it. Fuck me. I'm sorry I hurt you."

I kissed Savi and whispered to Emmi inside him, "Is that good?"

"Yeah, this is what I need. I need to cum. Arrrrgggggg." He yelled out. His face got red and he looked angry.

Savi picked up a rhythm. Quietly, you could hear Meijo take dick over and over as he was mechanically assaulted. He whispered "I'm. Sorry. I. Hurt. You. " over and over again in rhythm.

"Aaaah aaah aaah." With three massive pumps Savi started cumming, drilling him into the floor. Meijo screamed out and went immobile, that giant dick, anchored in his ass. Savi and Meijo were both crying. I got up and walked over to Rik. After a few minutes, Emmi pulled Savi's cock out of Meijo's poor hole and we could see how bad he was gaping. She turned him over and laid down with him stroking his hair. I wrapped Luna's body around Rik while the two of them laid on the ground kissing through tears, apologizing to each other for every invasion and pain that came with really wanting something.

***

"We look like the cast of a gangbang and we're going to meet this poor woman." Rik wasn't wrong. I had gotten Mika's address from the file, but really no other pertinent information.

"Hey, she's a girl. She's my age- 24. No women here. And, yes, we're just going to see if she can tell me any more about the accident or the trust fund or anything." Walking with the Luna body was so much easier, as I had anticipated. We had gotten off the tube and walked this last half mile, just because we could.

"Do you remember anything more in that body?" Meijo felt odd, I know, holding Luna's hand. But forced him. I loved watching people see him with Luna. I wanted people to see Luna fucking WORSHIPPING him. I wanted guys to wonder how he got so lucky that this beautiful woman would do anything for him. It was such a powerful thing and something I could never do as myself.

"I actually do. My parents passed before the accident. I remember that. I remember the hospital afterward. And there was one other person. We were in different rooms."

"Is that this Mika person?" Savi asked.

"I think so."

"And she has a trust fund, too?"

We stopped in front of a giant dement building with a fence. Inside looked like a first, surrounding a glass covered bright structure. It was beautiful and ostentatious and it probably cost a fortune.

"Yep."

At 5'8" Mka was a tallish handsome black girl. She opened the door in a band t-shirt and a pair of jeans. Opening the door, she seemed to take a shine to me in the Luna body immediately, suggesting where her interests lay. She invited us in for drinks.

Her place was massive. There were pictures all around featuring with her with various girls, but she seemed to live here alone.

She pulled out a tray of drinks. "So you guys want to know about the accident?"

I lifted my drink. Some fruity blue thing with a rim covered in sugar. It was fantastic, actually.

"I do. I had an accident on the same day."

"Do you remember yours?"

"I do not."

"And you have a trust fund, too?

"Yep, just like you. And I just found out who is paying into it?"

Mika looked up. She was honestly surprised. "Really?" he reached over and pulled up a picture on her wall monitor. "This is my parents. They died right before the accident."

Meijo looked over at me sharply. Was that too much of a coincidence?

"I was raised by an aunt I never met before. She said that I wasn't supposed to remember."

"See, what does that even mean?"

"I think it fucked with my memory, somehow. But it's good i don't remember. Like she said, even if I did remember, I should never talk about it."

Savi jumped in, "But what do you think it was?"

She didn't seem very interested in men. But she did use that as an opportunity to hold my hand. "I don't know anything about it. But that could be for the best."

"What if it's important that we find out." I used Luna's charms to try and make my way past Mika's defenses. She leaned in close to me.

"And what if it just makes everything worse?"

We talked with Mika for a bit. I had a feeling I could get more out of her, but it seemed like a lost cause. She walked us to the door.

"I'll see you soon?" I put my hand on her waist. She did the same.

"I hope so."

We stepped out the door and walked to the gate.

Meijo started, "ok, who here thinks she knows more than she's saying, raise your hand."

Even I put my hand up for that one. Savi looked at me.

"What are we going to do about that?"

"I stopped and put one finger up. "I'm going to improvise."

I walked back to the door and knocked. I leaned in and kissed Mika on the lips. She put her hand on the back of Luna's head and kissed me back, hard. There was something about her that felt different. Something that was intriguing. And the thought that she knew more was even more intriguing. I leaned in

"Do you want to be my date for a sex party tonight?"

***

Rik started tearing through Bron's computer back at the Den. I was trying to make some snacks but i admit that all i could think about was fucking while in the Luna body. And Emmi was no better. Both Meijo and I had sucked Savi off since we'd been back. I had no idea how one body could have that much cum in it. Rik asked me to grab my toothbrush and come over.

"So this is you, Seka, and no one else is using it?"

"No, I haven't used it on Luna yet."

"Good. hold on."

Rik's brother Eiko was already there for the party. I leaned in to watch what Rik was doing on the computer while Eiko fingered Luna's asshole.

"So, check this out." He started. On Bron's computer, I could see visualizations of DNA.

"These are the DNA charts for the Luna and Savi bodies."

I looked. "Ok, they look different."

"They are. All the phenotypic characteristics. The stuff you see, height, weight, eye color, etc."

"Is this what your students learn?" I laughed.

My students don't learn anything. They are tiny fucking morons."

"Got it."

"Now, see this area?" He selected a big range. It was identical.

"Yes. what is that?"

"Those are called introns. Junk DNA. it's other stuff that accumulates in your genes from your family. That's how we can tell where you are from, etc."

"ok. "

"And in the Luna and Savi bodies, they are identical."

"So they are..."

"They are clones, basically, of the same person, essentially."

"How? " I leaned back into Eiko's hand and let him work Luna's holes.

"I don't know, but they are essentially related."

"Ugh. that's not good. I was going to fuck that one later."

"They're both sterile so it won't matter."

"Good. no flipperbabies."

"It's weird, though. See, this is me and Eiko" he showed two other DNA strands.

"Ok, look how handsome that DNA is."

"Definitely, " Eiko chimed in.

"We're similar here and here and our introns are similar. But nowhere near as close as those LifeQuest Bodies."

"So they are totally artificial. And there is nothing there about the accident?" I think I got it.

"No. But there is one weird thing," Rik continued.

This was exciting. Weird. "What is it?"

"Now, see, this is you, Seka. This is your DNA. From your toothbrush. Now here are the Lifequest bodies. You see this." He outlined an area in all three chains.

"So I have some similar DNA?"

"Nope. Not just similar like me and this pervert here. The same. Exactly the same."

"Shit. So what does that mean."

"If I had to say what that means I would say something fucked up."

"What? What is it?"

"These bodies are partial clones of you. Of Seka Ogurd."

"Fuck."

Now I wanted to know what Mika knew, more than ever. There was something interesting about her- something hard to pin down. I figured that tonight was really about Emmi and that massive dick of hers so I could spend more time with Mika.

Emmi and Meijo seemed to have bonded a lot over the last couple of days' physical trauma as I watched them make out on the couch. The Savi body was so huge it looked like he could crush us all. It was hard to remember that there was a little girl in there.

Eiko wanted to just go in the other room and ride Luna for a while before we started so I took his hand and went into the front bedroom. This body was so light that it could do things I never thought of before. He lifted me up and swung me around, burying his face in luna's pussy while my head dangled down letting me pull his cock into my mouth.

I wrapped my arms around him and tried to get his big black dick deep into the back of my throat while he sucked on this body's sensitive clit and wide open wet cunt. He was able to hold me like that for a while as he sucked at me.

This was a good position for me to slide his thick dick up my throat without having to do any work. We played for a while.

I curled my knees around his head and came in his face, waiting for his cum in the back of my throat. He walked over to the bed and dropped forward onto it, crushing Luna under him in a way that drove his prick so deep into my mouth that I thought I could feel it in my chest. .

His full weight was on me while he dug his prick into my throat, letting his balls slap on my face every time his thrust came down. I held onto his ass and tried to pull him in deeper. I came on the bed, dripping out of Luna's pussy while Eiko lifted his ass and started pummelling my face with his cock, as though he were fucking a sex doll in the pussy.

His thick pelvis slammed into my face over and over and I could feel him lose control of everything and only think about his orgasm. I let my mouth and throat float open and sucked him in and let the rest of Luna's body fall loose, floppy against the bed.

He let out a grunt and grabbed the pussy with one hand, digging his fingers into Luna's cunt as he slammed into my face over and over. I could feel the bed bouncing hard as it began to move across the room in jittery limping movements, mirroring the twitching hammering of his massive dark dong into Luna's mouth.

With his other hand, he shoved his fingers up luna's ass and held the body down so he could continue. He lifted his ass and grunted now, louder with every thrust until he exploded into my mouth, digging his thick meat into my throat and holding it there while wave after wave of salty rich cum poured out of him into me. His hands were in both my ass and cunt now, pulling me down, keeping me from moving.

I held onto him, wrapping my arms around him and holding his ass as I drank it all in, filling Luna's belly with his hot load. We rocked back and forth like that for a while and I could tell he needed that.

A part of me thought about all the people that needed. If anything were true in the world it was that these people, the ones who needed, these were people I understood.

These were my people.

Party

I left Eiko sleeping in the bedroom and found MelJo in the Den. He looked like he needed some affection from me. He was wearing a shirt and no pants and I slid in next to him and held him. Emmi and Rik were wrestling hard in the pit and most of the rest of the room was just watching. I could tell that Maeijo had taken Savi's cock from Emmi at least one more time because his ass was still wide open. He had the slightly submissive demeanor that came over him when he was being topped well.

I slid four fingers of my left hand into his ass, cradling his balls. He was warm and slippery and I just massaged him while we kissed. Luna's hands were thinner than mine and luckily the nails were kept cut short. Her hands seemed like precision tools, delicate, caring. I put my other hand on the back of his neck and took some authority, opening his mouth under mine widely, digging my tongue as far into it as I could. He wrapped his arms around me lovingly and let them roam, playing with Luna's tightly muscled back and smooth, sleek belly.

There was no urgency in our makeout session, just a kind of melding together. In my head, I imagined that we were covered in slippery wet goo that was slowly hardening, pulling us together, making us into one body. My mouth tasted less and less like cum and more like him, his saliva dissolving and warming my lips. I pulled my hand out and licked it, covering it with my own saliva and slid it back into his asshole, a little deeper. He rearranged himself on the couch, opening up for me a little.

I pulled out slightly and slipped my thumb in, making that torpedo shape with my fist that is able to dig into holes like his.

Pushing him backward I kept kissing as his back sank into the couch. In My own body, my hand was a bit thicker, rounder. I was never able to get it inside him. In this body, it moved effortlessly in and I felt that tiny pop as my knuckles made it past his sphincter, opening him up. He let out a deep moan while I shifted onto my knees and kissed him deeply, arching over him.

We stayed like that for a while. His mouth was so wide open for me and I explored it with my tongue while I pulled my hand into a fist inside him. He let one leg fall over the back of the couch and put his hands over his head as if to say he trusted me. I'd never done this before and for a moment I tried to remember anything I knew about it. I wasn't sure how far I could push my fist safely. I looked down at his belly under me and pushed my hand against it. I could feel my fist moving slowly in and out if I pressed down on his belly. He moaned a little and I pushed further.

Did his stomach ripple from the movement of my fist, or was that my imagination?

I sat on my knees, getting leverage and realized that he still had space inside him. I advanced a little and he responded by widening his legs a tiny bit and groaning. I could see his cock, getting harder now, the head moving up and down slightly. I felt around inside him. I'd seen it in diagrams.

Pulling back a tiny bit, I suddenly felt what I thought might be his prostate. His belly shook a little and he moaned, suggesting I had it. I opened my hand a bit inside him and let my fingers play across it, watching his cock rise in the air. His balls looked tight and full and I realized he had been bottoming all day. Everyone was so fixated on Savi's enormous cock that Meijo had only been playing at being bottom.

His dick looked thick right now, ready. I could see the veins pop all over it, and they looked slightly blue against the ruddy bright olive red of it. A little river of white precum was running from the hole at the tip, down the groove of his head.

I realized that some of it had run down his balls and was currently smoothing out my entry into him. The idea that he was being fisted with his own cum was so hot to me that I became aware of my own cunt, throbbing between Luna's legs. I wished I had a bucket of his cum to pour into his own ass and fist him with, lubing him up with his own seed.

The more I played with his p-spot, the more he moaned, letting a steady small and pumping stream of jizz pour down his shaft. I wanted to lick it up, but I also wanted it to flow inside of him as badly as I also wanted it inside me. Some days, there is not enough cum in the world. At times like this, it's a gift that says you are where you should be, making a reality you want.

Thick white liquid pooled in the recess of his balls now, overflowing and lubricating his own invasion. It was a beautiful perpetual motion machine. I wondered how long I could milk him like this. Right now, he was my cow, my livestock, behaving for me so I could use him and milk him, taking what he had inside him. He was moving his hips slowly now, obediently, along with the movements of my arm. My fist must have been bigger than Savi's cock, but while that was pain and subjugation and violence, this was just loving submission to the will of his owner, just a pet opening up his body to his keeper's humiliating administrations, no matter how intimate or how medically invasive they might be.

This wasn't him having his will bent by a thick dick but just him giving away his everything for someone he loved who was obviously worth it, obviously his superior.

I thought about how he said he loved me while he was cumming inside Emmi and how, tonight, I would ask him to say it again cumming inside Luna, until, one day soon, he would be saying it cumming inside me.

The real me.

After he was drained, I licked up as much of him as I could, cleaning him off. He rolled over on the couch to sleep as I licked the last of it from his ass. I now had two separate men sleeping off what I did to them in two different rooms.

This party was a success already.

Rik and Savi were sucking each other in the pit now, like animals, both naked, looking for all the world like they were wrestling each other, each one thinking they were winning. It was vicious and wild. Emmi was really holding her own, in the giant Savi's body, pushing Rik down and trying to fuck his head into the floor.

I put on a white robe that hung delicately off of Luna's frame, secretly impressed with how well Emmi was rising to the role of He-Man. Just as I had slid the robe over my shoulders, the doorbell rang. Most of my friends just walked in the back way so there was only one person that could be.

I padded to the door and opened it, to find Mika on the other side, holding a bottle of wine. She looked at me in my thin robe hanging loosely over Luna's body.

"Damn, girl. You weren't kidding."

I flashed her. "I know, crazy, right?"

"Is this really a sex party?" She was walking down the hallway with me. She didn't seem timid.

I turned to her. "Ok, yes. But you don't need to do anything. You can just watch."

She grabbed my hand, "What if I just want to hang out with you?"

This level of flirty was only possible right now using Luna's body. I wondered if I could be flirty like this as myself with someone new. I looked at her eyes and saw her drilling into me.

Maybe I could if someone looked at the real me like that. I grabbed her hand and leaned in. She leaned forward to kiss me. She was tall. The first woman I'd seen in this body taller than me.

She kissed me harder than I expected. She put her hand behind me to hold my head and I opened my mouth to let her in. I could see that she was kind of dominant. I leaned against the wall and she followed, pushing in. I let the front of the robe fall open and rubbed the body against her, lifting one leg.

"You're really beautiful. She said, pulling back to look for a second. I put my arms around her and pulled her back into me. I tried to open my mouth wide, pliant, for her. Her skin was smooth and dark brown and sleekly pretty and her lips were wide and plump and inviting.

I liked the way she kissed. Her hands played over my tits and squeezed the nipples, maybe a little harder than I expected. She was forceful and I could feel the demand coming from her, the need. This was familiar to the Luna body.

And it was becoming more familiar to me.

She moved her hips, almost like she had a strap on, and I spread my legs. We pantomimed like she was fucking me up against the wall while I sucked on her lips and wrapped my arms tightly around her.

"Do you like me?" it seemed a weird time for her to ask me, but I recognized where it was coming from.

"Very much," and I did. She had something strong about her face. I realized, holding her close, that this was the closest I had ever come to knowing anything really about the accident.

But there was more than that. Something about her seemed really familiar. Like maybe we were even close, before the accident. Like we might have known each other.

I pulled the robe off completely. "Is there anything you want to do to this body?" I posed in front of her.

"Just like that, huh?" She smiled at me.

"Just like that." I took her hand and moved down the hallway to my room. I could hear activity in the den, but I figured that if she only wanted to hang out with me, this might fit her needs better.

"Your place is nice." She said, following me.

"Jesus, it's nothing like yours. I feel like I wasted my trust fund. Ha."

"My place is a bit more…"

I fell back on the bed and spread Luna's legs. "Demure?"

"Yeah, pretty much." She looked down at me and shook her head. "Amazing."

"I like your lips." I said, putting my hand between Luna's legs, fingering the clit."

She kneeled on the bed and crawled toward me. "I love your tattoos.

The tattoos running up and down Luna's arms were pretty, astronomical symbols. The moon factored in heavily with each. These were Luna's tattoos, tailored to her name, her body. They fit it perfectly.

"Do you have any tattoos," I tried, flirting. She leaned in and kissed me.

"Not a single one. I'm totally blank."

For a minute, that seemed hot to me. She was untouched in a way. "Hmmm. a tattoo virgin, huh?"

Mika laughed and pulled her shirt off. She had pretty and very round breasts on a broad chest that made her look so strong. Submitting to her wouldn't be hard. She had a body that seemed to demand obedience, in a classical sense. Thick and strong.

"I'm such a virgin." She countered, pulling my face in to kiss her breasts. I sucked at them eagerly as she pulled her pants down, kicking her jeans across the room. "Is this your room?"

"I mean, yes, the whole place is mine, But this is my bedroom." I technically lived here alone but the six bedrooms were often full with friends. Hell, Rik's was usually kept locked when he wasn't here.

"So I get to fuck a girl in her own bedroom on the first date?" she joked. I felt like we were getting close to a kind of role play.

"If you want to." I put my hands on her ass and sucked harder on her tits. "I'd love to be fucked by you on the first date."

"You want it pretty bad, huh?" She pulled me back a little by the hair and then pushed my head down to her belly. I licked at it, swirled my tongue in her belly button.

"I do. Please? Please fuck me on the first date."

Her underwear was black and cottony. She took one hand and shimmied out of them, pulling them off, while, with the other, she grabbed my head by the hair and pushed me down.

"Do you like that little dick?" She was totally shaved and had the prettiest thick lips around her pussy. But the first thing I saw was her clit, enlarged and full, poking out from her cunt at least an inch and a half. It was beautiful.

"Oh, I love it." I put my hands under her and grabbed her ass. I held her clit at the base and slid my lips over it.

"Oh, fuck, yeah." She pushed her hips forward and I felt like she wanted to fuck my face with it.

"So fucking hot." I pulled at it and it extended another half inch or so It was like a small dick, a prick that was 2 inches long, but perfect and waiting to explode.

I sucked it and tried to let m neck fall loose so Mika could fuck my face with it. I played with her lips but really focused on the growing clit in my mouth, trying to make her feel like I was giving her dick all the attention.

"Yeah, suck suck that. Suck my dick." She looked strong and focused.

I leaned into the role play hard. I massaged her clit, running my fingers up and down it, while I sucked it like a cock. "What a pretty fucking cock." I imagined it was growing even bigger and harder in my mouth as I took it in.

"Yeah. You suck dick so well." She looked down while I ministered to her prick, licking and sucking it.

I looked up wanting, "Mika, I want your dick so bad." I put my whole on it, licking and sucking it in. I could feel how wet she was getting, mixing with my saliva all over her. She tasted steamy and rich and full. Her dick felt alive.

"C'mon, girl. Suck it. Come here." She grabbed my head and held it, almost like a bowling ball, rubbing herself on my face, burying that clit deep into my mouth. I tried to drink up the wet from her, leaking from her cunt, as I held onto her ass and let her use Luna's face to get off.

She got on top of me and pressed downward, leaning against the wall behind the bed and driving her massive clit into my face over and over. She stopped talking and just let her hips push my head into the bed over and over again.

Harder and harder she bounced, dripping all over into my mouth while she used Luna's face. She held onto her tits and jammed her ass as hard as possible downward, drenching me, until she finally came, loudly, letting her cock rest in my mouth, her pelvic bone digging into my face.

I massaged her ass while she leaned against the wall, spent. I slowly licked the liquid from under her and waited until she slid down the lay next to me.

"Was that weird?" She whispered.

"It was hot weird," I laughed, in Luna's melodic voice.

She looked over at me. "You are so pretty. You sort of look familiar."

"Oh, you look very familiar." I thought about how this body shared some similarities with my own, from the long black hair to the pouty lips and brooding eyebrows.

But it was so much better.

I was beginning to process what it felt to be wanted like this.

I knew that Meijo wanted me, although I was beginning to be able to process that better. And I knew that friends like Rik and Emmi wanted me enough to play a little here and there. But here, at this party, was a house full of people who wanted me so much- this body so much - that they could barely control themselves.

I burrowed in next to Mika and closed my eyes for a minute. I tried to time my breathing to hers as I felt her drifting off to sleep.

In the dark, I tried to connect with Luna again. It was stupid. I knew this was just a body. But there was that weird spark before. And the vision. I felt around in my head. It was true, I did feel less foggy in this body. It's almost like there was a haze lifted. I was able to think a little better, when I dug back into my past.

I heard Luna's voice in my head telling me to get up. It was strange because even though I now, in this body, spoke with Luna's voice, this was different. It was a different speaker. I sat up and looked down at Mika.

The voice said, "Run."

I shot out of bed and made my way into the Den. It was a little darker now, and I could see that outside, the day had ended. There were about 15 people in the den now, cuddling and talking, most in various states of undress. I moved over to the bar where Meijo and Rik were leaning, drinking, sliding into Meijo's arms. It was strange, in this body, being the same height as he was. He kissed me and put his hands on Luna's ass.

"Are you ok?"

"Yes. I just got spooked a bit. Mika is here."

Rik looked over, "Damn. She actually came."

I smiled. "She did. And she did." Meijo laughed. Our friend Layla was sucking off Emmi in Savi's body on the couch languidly. I pointed, "And that fucking thing is still going, huh?"

Rick grunted. Meijo responded. "It's insane. He's come like ten times."

I saw his eyes move first. And then I heard it from behind me.

"Hey,"

We all turned. Mika was in the entryway of the Den. She yelled out again, "Hey!" in one hand she held up a pulse gun. She was still topless, in her black underwear. In the other hand was a picture of Seka. Of me.

"Who is this? She waved the gun around. "Who the fuck is this?"

She must have woken up and found the picture in my room. Savi was up incredibly fast, buck naked, just as I was, and before I knew it he was right there, covering me on one side while Meijo leaned in, right in her line of sight. Rik waved his hands, "Calm down."

"Don't tell me to fucking calm down. Where is she? Where is this girl?"

I started to move forward to tell her it was me. Meijo held me back. "Why do you want her?"

"Where the fuck is she. She ruined my life. She stole my fucking life." She pointed the gun.

Some of the people in the room looked over at me. She noticed and swung the gun right at my head.

"Is this you? Are you this fucking girl? What the fuck?" She raised the gun and let off two pulses from the gun. Savi ran toward her and made a move to tackle her. Just as his body slammed into her chest, she had released one more pulse, with the gun pointed directly at her head.

I looked over at Savi. Under him was Mika's body, with a piece of her head missing. He was holding his side, where a hole had appeared. I went to take a step toward him but I couldn't.

I looked down. There was a hole through the body's abdomen. And smoke was coming from it. I put my hand over it.

"Fuck."

And fell over.

Baja

"So, your life is a lot more interesting than I thought." Bron had a replacement computer and seemed to be enjoying our new relationship. Emmi and I were putting our clothes on while he watched. He folded his arms and let a huge grin wash across his face.

"Are the bodies going to be ok?" I felt shitty about a lot of things, but hurting Luna and Savi was up there toward the top.

"They... will be fine." He finished typing and spun around in his chair. "It's going to take about a week to heal those injuries but you won't even see a scar."

"Really?" Emmi was amazed. I could tell she was feeling some way from being in her own body again. I wondered if she felt the reverse of how I felt, going from Savi's massive body to her tiny frame. Did she feel like she might suddenly float away?

"Did you get what you needed from the computer?" Bron looked us over. I'm sure he enjoyed watching us while we were gone. This might have been his way of conjuring up the image in our heads - recalling the deal. He wanted us to imagine him looking at us. Human sexuality is recursive.

I breathed out. "Not yet. I have things I'm trying to figure out."

"Like what?" he asked. "Why don't you ask me? I know things about LifeQuest."

I looked at his ruddy face and decided. No, I did not yet trust him.

"Let me think about it."

"Well, do that. And, if you are interested, I do have a body I think you'll love. For next time. It's stunning."

I turned to him. I tried to screw up my courage. In the Luna body, this would be easy and I would come across so cool.

Do you want to see something sweet?"

He nodded. I turned to Emmi.

"Can I kiss you for trying to save me?"

She smiled and hopped off the table where she had been tying her boots. She nodded at me and came over. This seemed kind of big to me and I had no idea why. I looked down. She was so tiny and thin. And her body just smelled good, despite being on that table for two days.

She lifted my chin and leaned in, her mouth opening. I closed my eyes and fell into the kiss. Her lips were soft and wet and not at all urgent. She didn't pull away or try to close her mouth so I left mine open, too, flicking at her tongue with my own. She wrapped her arms around me.

And we kissed in front of him for a long time.

***

I walked with Emmi and Meijo the mile to Rik's work. I rarely walked in my own body and it just seemed like too good a day to miss out. I also realize that I felt trapped a lot lately. I really rarely left my own place. I'd designed it to sort of be a womb for me and maybe it was time to get born a little.

"So, I was unconscious. The police don't have a huge issue with the tall black rich woman who tried to kill us and then inexplicably shot herself?"

Emmi almost skipped along the street in the warm Baja air. She clearly felt lighter.

Meijo interjected. "Well, there were about 15 witnesses with the exact same story. And the LifeQuest people showed up before the police.

Emmi found that amusing, "They are on it."

They were. I was trying to feel as light as she was. We dodged a bullet. I mean I, *myself*, dodged a bullet. I could have been killed. "I must have really done something awful to her."

"Or," Meijo added, "She was a really messed up person. Can I ask you something?"

I grabbed his hand and turned. "Yes. Please. Ask a smart question that makes sense of some of this."

"What do *you* think the accident was?"

I thought about that. There were a series of metal benches set up all across the walkways in Baja. They were recently put up by the newer, more progressive government to make the streets more open, more filled with life. And they worked. It was kind of nice to see people having fun. I sat down. People having fun is my jam.

"I was too young to drive. So that's out. I don't think I shot anyone. I mean, how did I ruin someone's life? I can't imagine I was violent. I'm just not like that. If I hurt anyone, it couldn't have been on purpose. And why would some biotech company care enough to spend a literal fortune to keep it quiet?"

Emmi played with my hair. This, too, was my jam. If this was payback for the kiss, I was all over it. I leaned into it and hoped she noticed.

"Was there anything about her that you could use as a clue? Anything different?"

"Yeah, anything that kickstarted a memory, maybe?"

"I did kind of remember her face. But smaller? She was a normal person. I mean, she was a bit of a pervert, like all of us. I feel like we might have been friends. I mean, you saw her. " I thought hard.

"You talked with her. Did *you* see any red flags? It was normal."

"But then, something happened..." Meijo prodded.

"And I ruined her life forever and she killed herself." I finished. If I thought too much about this, it was crushing. It was like a massive weight. What did I do?

"That's not on you. None of it's on you." Emmi was more serious than I'd ever seen her. I didn't want her to be serious on my account.

"Ok, enough of my issues. How do YOU feel?"

Emmi closed her eyes and thought. "I feel really strange. Like most of the last couple days was a dream. I feel light and floaty and little. I feel vulnerable. But, there is so much I loved. And so much more to do. I feel really close to you guys. I got to really rearrange some guts. And then my own got rearranged a bit."

"Epic." Meijo laughed.

"And next time, I want to try wearing the Luna body. What do you think?"

I hadn't considered that but then realized that if she did, that I could have sex with Luna. That sounded amazing. "Oh, my god, that's a brilliant idea."

Emmi squealed. This was her happy. I tried to let go of what had happened with Mika. Figuring it all out was one step to doing that.

I leaned back in the metal seat. I tried to forget that I watched someone die last night. For no reason I could figure out. It was just weird and pointless and still, somehow, my fault. But we were halfway to Rik's work.

Maybe he could help.

***

"I can not help."

"Well, don't sugar coat it, man." I grabbed an orange off of the bowl in front of him and started peeling.

"It's all information. That's all there is. And before twelve years ago, there was no information for Mika Spencer, some information for Seka Ogurd but nothing interesting, no information for half the people in these files. And these go back twenty years. twenty years of people just being invented out of thin air or mostly invented."

Emmi grabbed an apple. "Is it ok for us to be here?" She waved behind her at the room full of about fifty students reading, talking, and occasionally sleeping their way through his class."

"Oh, these? They're already all getting an F for the day. Little weasels." He said that last part loudly at them.

"Damn." Meijo grabbed half of my orange and started eating it. "Tough room."

"So, am I a clone, like those bodies?"

"No. The bodies are clearly clones based on a comparison of introns and their extant parasites. One of the reasons cloning is weird is that birth creates a new entity, with a new "lock" that the existing parasites have to evolve to "key" open."

"Right. So, not a clone."

"But your DNA is definitely being used in the clone bodies."

"Without my permission."

"They're basically paying you a fortune." Meijo finished his stolen orange half.

"We don't know why, do we?"

Rick shook his head. "No, nothing."

Emmi looked up, "Hey, you said twenty years."

"Yeah, give or take…"

"So what was the first one? For P-Ref-LQ77," she read. "Who was first?"

"It's her." Rik swung his computer around. It was a very pretty Black girl with cornrows. She was smiling, holding a baby. "The winner and reigning champion is Cerrone Michaels."

"Ok. that is fantastic. Queen." I actually felt like we had a lead. Maybe.

"And one more thing. I think, based on Baja state records, that your unhinged woman had a brother. Nothing for her, but something for him."

"How do you know?"

State records have a Michael Spencer living about a block away from your childhood home. Apparently, when he was 10 years old, he won some scholarship. Then, he disappeared."

So, maybe two leads.

***

Hundreds of years ago, Baja was a state torn between two countries. It's a peninsula, and it was attached to the bottom of Old California, an American state. But it sat right across a gulf from Sonora, a Mexican one and was part of the country of Mexico. In the middle of the Great loss, it became a country all on its own. And the people were very independent. They believed very strongly in personal freedoms and in autonomy. So, during this time, it actually became a bit of an oasis, a place where things never really fell apart quite as badly as they did elsewhere.

It didn't hurt that it was temperate, surrounded by beautiful water and beaches, and had a wealth of its own farming and orchards. The running joke during bad times was that anything would grow in Baja.

When the United States began to pull itself together again, the movement started on the west coast and was driven by building out a new progressive model for governance, one that valued information and education. And Baja was the fourth state to join, after Oregon, South California and North California.

Now, Baja had never really fallen apart as hard as many other locations. In fact, much of it stayed afloat when the world went to hell. And for at least 100 years, it's been building on infrastructure.

In comparison, most of the rest of the seventeen states of the New United states are just rebuilding much of their information infrastructure. To say that Baja has two entirely separate sort of databases that describe the patterns and behaviors of its people would be a wise observation. One of them is old school and kept up by federal employees, most of which are fairly new to this job of maintaining a sixty year old country.

And one is a little more high tech, and is owned by the state of Baja, a state that has been engaged in managing the comings and goings of its people during the hundred years when it was a standalone country.

Those two databases don't always agree. In fact, they agree only in the most simple of situations.

And that's how Rik got the impression that there were two Spencer children, one named Michael, who disappeared, and the other named Mika who appeared, both happenings being on July 17th 2487. This was the date of my accident, an event I had no first hand knowledge of except the put-upon realization that I had ruined someone's life enough to make them shoot me and then themselves in the middle of my Den.

I tell you this in hindsight, after the four of us found ourselves in Ensenada at the Spencer home Where Mika Spencer's grandparents now lived holding a mass card with a small obituary and a childhood picture of Mika Spencer that was being given away to neighbors...

Mourning the loss of their grandson.

About twelve hours ago.

"That looks like the same person." Emmi held it up to the light.

"Well…" Meijo looked at me and rubbed my neck. "Nope, I got nothing."

"Mystery solved. You were playing around learning how to throw knives and you cut his dick off. Michael becomes Mika, vows revenge, Lifequest's knife manufacturing department tries to make it go away."

"I do not like this story." I didn't like that story.

"First up, I don't think Lifequest makes Knives. I mean, I know it's part of the joke, but…" Emmi handed me the picture.

Looking at it, I was closer to recognizing it. Then something occurred to me.

"I think he's cute."

Rik looked over my shoulder, "He's a handsome kid."

"No, I mean, I think that 12 year old me would have wanted to date him, to be his girlfriend or something. I think we were more than friends."

"You can tell that from a picture? "Meijo asked."

"Look, if someone wiped my memory and showed me your picture, i would be like 'yeah, I wanted that guy's dick in me somewhere.'" I put my hand under his face, "I mean, look at this little face."

"It's a good face." Emmi jumped in. "So, you're maybe dating this guy, something bad happens, he ends up as a woman, you end up traumatized…"

"But I saw Mika naked. Is there an operation that good?"

"Was there anything unusual?" Rik tried to move us away from people who might overhear.

"She actually did seem to be kind of masc. She wanted me to treat her clit like a dick. And it was long."

"Hot," Emma interjected. It was actually hot how many things she thought were hot.

"Something she did on her own, to emulate lost masculinity?" Rik offered.

"That could be."

Meijo stopped and turned around. "Look, I'm going to make a suggestion." He grabbed my hand and held up the picture with the other one. "We put this picture down right here. We walk away from it. We put that computer away and put those files in a cabinet. Then we pretend there is no mystery. If all this is about trying to figure out some accident you had twelve years ago, who cares, really? Do you need to know? We have a life that's good. If it's about why you seem to have some mental block against penetration, who cares? You're getting closer to getting over that everyday just by playing. And if you never get there all the way, fine. Great. No biggie."

I won't lie. What he said made a ton of sense. In a lot of ways, I had a pretty perfect present. And it was getting better. Did I want to waste my time trying to find a past that didn't seem all that great to start with?

The hot guy made a compelling argument. I mean, it was my fault that we had tracked down Mika Spencer and she broke down the way she did. I probably ruined her life then was responsible for her death. If I'd just kept my eyes open looking forward, she'd be alive.

I turned to look at everyone. Rik was really doing everything in his power to help me figure stuff out even though there was nothing in it for him. Emmi and Meijo were being better friends than they needed to be. And I was currently just dragging this whole train downward.

"Ok. Who here would rather grab a literal shitload of chinese food, bring it home and stuff our faces all night that spend time pursuing a deep traumatic piece of my childhood past? Raise your hands."

Emmi's hand shot in the air and she jumped up and down.

Meijo and Rik looked at me and raised their hands.

And the answer was Chinese.

***

Later, we walked into a perfectly clean home. I keep forgetting I have a maid because I literally *never saw her*. It's a very odd thing. She came with the house and I tried to get to know her for the first few months until I realized she was hiding from me. She was one of those hyper professionals who believed that if I ever saw her she must be failing in her job.

So she must have cleaned up blood and god knows what other body fluids without complaining and then disappeared. Whatever I was paying her was not enough.

I pressed a button and the transparent table in the pit expanded a little wider. I put the egg fu yung in the center of the table, followed by other dishes I would not be eating. I really was a sort of single dish chinese food eater.

Emmi looked really happy. During the time she was wearing the Savi body, I realized I had missed her face. "I have no idea what a chinese is, but I love the food."

Rik looked over, "Em, I actually think you are Chinese."

"Nofuckingway," she spit out, grabbing an egg roll

Yes, it's true that there was no country named China anymore and hadn't been one for about 300 years. But that didn't make the food disappear. Or stop people from being of Chinese ancestry. It did, apparently, cause them to not connect the two.

"So, wait, my people invented moo shu pork?" she asked, grabbing a pancake.

Rick shook his head, "I think you're fucking with me."

***

This was the beginning of two straight weeks of play, both with and without LifeQuest Secondbodies. This is important, I think, because it may help explain what happens afterward. That day, I stopped trying to dig too hard into what had happened to me.

I stopped trying to revisit this every day and build a past for myself, sinking every day a little more comfortably into my present. I stopped trying to figure out if what had happened in the past had any real impact on who I was. In fact, I stopped trying to figure out who I was at all.

Until I had to figure out *what* I was.

Body

We all slept in the back bedroom with the giant "superbed." Superbed filled one entire side of the room and it was always a dream of mine when I was younger.

It was starting to come in handy.

Rik had left for work and Meijo was getting some painting done. I was lying under a couple of covers watching Emmi doing a pretty deep split and then bending forward. She was remarkably bendy. I'd been watching for about 10 minutes and the fact that she was bottomless, wearing only a thin black see-through shirt wasn't helping me get back to sleep.

"Is there any reason you can think of why you can't be doing that on my face?"

"Well. I'm all sweaty and I actually have to pee."

My brain surged. "Oh wow. You really aren't helping. Bad reasons."

She laughed and pulled herself up. She walked over to the bed. "Are you sure?"

"I want to be your workout bench." I flopped backward and put my arms out while she climbed on the bed.

Facing my legs she gingerly pressed her cunt and ass against my face and then leaned back, her whole weight falling on my face. She spread her legs and did a perfect split, her legs making a line across the bed. Bending forward, she put her hands on my belly and tried to reach them with her head.

My mouth and nose fit perfectly into the space made by her tiny pink pussy and asshole, open and sweaty, wet for me. I kept my mouth open and made my lips into a seal around her cunt, catching her juices as she exercised, moving up and down with precision. I let my tongue wander around the inside of her pussy as I drunk in the smell of her, warm and musky and perfect.

My tongue played across her inner lips and then, finally, found the tiny puckered hole sitting in front of her vagina and behind her clit. I teased it while she grunted on top of me.

I'd never done this with a woman before. I always imagined that if I wanted to get a woman to piss in my mouth I'd softly insert the tip of my tongue into her urethra, opening it up, making it ready to release for me. I didn't realize how open and soft it would be. I felt like I could fuck it with my tongue.

"Oh, that feels good. That feels so weird." she pushed down a little harder and my tongue pushed a little deeper into her tiny hole.

"That's a different thing. It feels so different. But I don't think I can do it."

I held her down now, wrapping my hands around her waist and pulling. Her spaces were warm and wet like a little sauna. Her skin was hot from movement and I felt it all over my face.

My hands were slippery with her sweat and I wished I could lick them. I dug my nose into her ass and worked harder on her little hole in front.

"Ok. I think I'm going to pee." she whispered. The fact that she was whispering turned me on endlessly. I don't know why. But she stopped her slow rocking movements and anchored her hands on me as if she were concentrating.

I opened my mouth as widely as I could, making a tight seal around her pussy. It started slowly, just a few drops. And then it built. I pulled her close and clamped my lips, making sure she knew I wanted it. I swallowed quickly and let it fill me as the stream got thicker and more dense.

I tried not to choke or do anything that might make her stop for a moment, anything to let her know I wanted her to keep going. She moaned and let go and a torrent of piss filled my mouth in one long wave. I could feel her breathe out in release.

I sucked at her, drinking it all and cleaning her cunt with my tongue. I cleaned off her clit, rubbing my tongue on it and she moaned a little and leaned forward, pressing her head against my stomach. Her pose made her feel so open as I sucked and licked at her cunt, and I could feel her lips fill up and get thicker, rubbing against my face.

She pushed against my face and let her legs fall backwards a bit, closing in around my head while she rubbed her little button on my mouth. She was moaning a lot now and I could feel her getting ready to cum and I kept at it, pulling her closer to me and digging my nails into her ass. She finally twitched and spasmed on my face and there was a little pool of liquid that filled the space in her cunt, one just for me.

I held her close as she laid there breathing and thought about going back to sleep, wearing her on my face like a mask.

She rolled off me and laid down next to me, pulling me over to cuddle. She kissed me hard, the taste of her piss still in my mouth, letting her saliva overwhelm it and take it away. "This has been a crazy week.

I turned to her, "ok, what did you like, what didn't you like?"

She closed her eyes and thought for a second. "I liked it all. I liked being a detective, but that's nothing. We can do that for anything. I like sometimes..."

She pulled herself up on her elbows and explained, "It's strange. With all of you, I don't have that feeling that I'm just a body that's not good enough. So, I feel safe. And noticed.

And because of that, I sometimes just want to BE a body, to be used. Like, I liked being your body, for you. And then using you as a body,. And then using the Savi body, using other people with that. It's weird. But it's simple. Sometimes we're the object, sometimes we're the brain. And if we are both, then we're both, you know?"

Strangely, I DID know. I did understand. Because sometimes I want to be the thing that people forget about while they're having fun, intensely. And then, right afterward, be the thing they are so intensely focused on they don't see anything else. To be useful and then to be inevitable. To be a thing and then...

Magically...

To be everything.

And I was on this journey to be a body that can be used completely. And I actually felt like I had company. I kissed her hard, running my hands over her. It was going to be a little bit until we could use Luna again.

"Do you want to be the body or the brain today?"

***

It had been a couple days since, in the Luna body, someone had put their hand inside me to play with Eiko's cock. I'd been thinking a lot since then. And now I had a body to work with.

Meijo was sitting in the deon, drawing in the pit. Emmi was so little, I could practically carry her around. I had put the collar and leash around her neck and it did make things easier.

I dragged her over to where he sat. I noticed that if I put a few fingers in her ass and then lifted her that way, with my other hand on the collar, I could control her fairly well.

"Good morning to you, too," Meijo put down the pad as I smashed Emmi's mouth into his crotch. She was quiet but I could hear her moan a little when I pushed my hand deeper up her ass. She was like a puppet, I mused.

Meijo pulled his pants down and his cock sprung up. I lifted Emmi's head onto it and shoved her face down hard, until the entire thing was gone, missing down her throat. I moved her up and down slowly on his dick and gave him a kiss, "I missed you this morning."

He leaned back a bit. "Hm. that feels good."

"Is that a good speed?"

"It's great. Fuck." He half closed his eyes.

"Ok. I've been wanting to give you a morning hand job, but I want to do it through her. Is that cool?"

He nodded, "That's great." I could hear her grunt a bit. I had asked her earlier how intense she wanted it. And when she said ten, I asked her again. I was hoping she understood what a ten was.

"This should hurt her a lot but feel good for you, is that cool?"

"Like when she fucking raped my ass with that massive dick?"

"Probably worse."

"I still feel that fucking dong up inside me. It's like phantom cock. "

"I'm sorry, baby." I pushed her head down harder on his dick. She was choking and spitting up. It was beautiful.

"Can she take it?"

"Oh, yeah. This body is tough. It can take anything we do to it today.

"Do you think she'll learn her lesson?"

"Probably not. The minute she has a prick again, she's probably going to be a total bitch about it. Hold on"

I jammed her head down one last time then lifted her up. Her face was wet and messy and she was breathing hard. I spit in her face a few times then wiped it all up with my hand, rubbing it all into her asshole, already partially opened from my hand. Lifting her up, I sat her in Meijo's lap, his prick sliding up her back way. She breathed in sharply as I pushed her down as far as she would go, Her ass impaled on his cock.

She was breathing and sputtering hard, spit dripping from her mouth.

"Ah. Fuck, yeah. Is everything ok?"

"Yeah." I slapped her chest a couple times and then pulled back and slapped her face. "Just trying to get the body to behave a little.

She was making tiny noises, her breathing quick and sharp. She said something softly.

I pulled back and slapped her hard over and over in rhythm, "Shut! The! Fuck! Up!"

"This body feels good."

"I hope it doesn't fuck this up. I just wanted to give you a nice hand job."

Emmi's face looked so pretty now. It was all read and wet and there were tears in her eyes. I grabbed her by the throat and pushed down.

Kneeling down in front of them, I took my other hand and shoved it in her cunt. She gasped and started breathing hard as I pushed it upward, laying it against the back wall of her vaginal canal. Even with just a few fingers in, I could feel Meijo's cock through the thin walls inside her.

"Can you feel my hand?" He nodded. "I'm going to try to grab your dick."

Emmi looked frantic, letting out a little whine. Her eyes widened in the understanding that this would hurt. I slapped her again.

And that's when her body betrayed her. A rush of cum poured out of her pussy as she closed her eyes, her ass battered by Meijo's prick, her face assaulted by my slaps.

"Did you feel that?" I asked Meijo

"Yeah, that was nice and warm on my balls."

I reached into her more easily now. My hand was not tiny but it slid in far enough that I could feel a good 4 inches or so of the cock as it rammed its way through her anal cavity. Emmi started to moan loudly as I closed my hand a little around Meijo's dick, grabbing it through her inner divider. Suddenly, I was in, and the space was supple, giving. I closed my hand a little more, and started rubbing the rod up her ass back and forth, fisting her at the same time. She let out a scream and, with the other hand, I resumed choking her. "Shut up."

I thought about her kicking me with her beautiful boots on and I spit in her face again. Sometimes it's hard to tell why you do these things. Was I trying to push her so that the next time I was bent over in front of her she would take it out on me? A spark between my legs suggested to me that was true. I could tell by the river from between *her* legs that she was enjoying it. I tried to make myself not care, visibly, to show her that.

"Is that good, baby?"

"Oh, your hand feels so good."

"Are you going to dump some cum in this hole for me?"

"I will baby. I will."

I leaned in and kissed him. "I like to get your pretty dick off. Is there anything more I can do, baby."

Meijo closed his eyes. "Just don't stop. Don't stop…"

I pushed harder, jacking him off while he was inside the body's ass. She was moving back and forth hard, holes filled and aching. I loved that people could yell all they wanted to at my place without being heard.

And she did.

I could feel her cumming on my hand just as Meijo let loose up her asshole.

She screamed and leaned back against him. Meijo wrapped his arms around her and we both kissed her face. He pulled her head back and kissed her open mouthed for a few minutes. I waited and then pulled her down by the collar.

And the two of us licked his cock clean, sucking up all the cum from his lap.

Rik appeared in the entryway with Eiko and our friend Tanya, who had been at the last party wIth her girlfriend.

I looked up smiling.

"Well, y'all are clearly not watching the news." Rik pointed his phone at the far monitor wall and it shifted. '

"And the changes will be far reaching, I'm sure." There was a handsome woman in a suit coat with short pretty red hair speaking in front of what looked like an official building. "To recap the big story, the Oregon Plurality Council has been won in a landslide by Senza Dolore. They say there are no plans yet to eject men from the state, but many pundits say to watch out. This will be the first state to cede both houses to The international Senza Dolore party but are they the last?"

He pulled the volume down. I really was in my own bubble here.

Meijo pulled a blanket over his waist. "Wow. That is insane. That's two states away."

"Two giant states," Tanya sat down. She was a tall red haired girl. I didn't know her that well but I did kiss her in the luna body. I didn't know if she remembered.

That would never happen here, in Baja?" Eicko gave me a quick kiss then plopped down next to all of us. This is what the pit was meant for. I liked it when it was full of people.

Emmi sat down crosslegged, pulling some of Meijo's blanket over her. "I don't know. I mean, why do I feel like it's so different here?"

I thought, "In Baja. weird. I think of it as different. Maybe it's the people we know."

Rik sighed, "Well, men have been pretty brutal all over. For a long time."

"But you guys are more like girls."

"Meijo laughed, "Well, allright."

"What do you think that means?" I went to go get some drinks from the little bar. Meijo jumped up to go with.

Eicko looked around. "I think it means we're cool."

Meijo shot back, "And maybe I'm kind of pretty."

Rik acknowledged it, smiling. "Yeah, he's pretty, whatever."

"It's simple." Emmi pointed out. "She says you're like girls and you guys all think of it as a compliment because you innately think women are cool and you respect them."

Meijo handed Tanya a beer and she took a sip. "Right, like it's not an insult for you."

"Honestly, it's a load off my back." Rik took a beer and opened it. "To not be a MAN. You know? There is so much bullshit that comes with that. It's historical bullshit."

"It's like being a virus trying to figure out how not to be contagious." Eiko offered up. This was painful to hear. But I understood.

"There is some correcting that has to happen. And this could be part of it." Meijo gave Emmi a drink and sat back down.

It was scary to think about how much correcting might need to happen. "Like women in charge for a while?"

Eiko laughed, "like maybe a long while. It's been thousands of years of rule by men. To 900 years of women rule." He toasted. We all joined in.

Tanya looked at him, "And you're not afraid of that?"

"I don't think it's something that will oppress men. It's not about that. It's about safety. And I'm not afraid of that at all. This is what that looks like" He pointed to Meijo and Emmi naked drinking on the couch."

"Safety is people drinking naked in a giant opulent house in a massive overstuffed conversation pit?" Tanya had actually talked herself into that as she went on. "Honestly, as I say it... You're not wrong."

We laughed. We talked politics deep into the night. It was one of those conversations where people just fade off and fall asleep where they're sitting.

I got up in the middle of the night and everyone was asleep. Tanya was crashed with her feet over Rik's lap and Emmi and Meijo were cuddled, still naked, at the end of the couch.

I grabbed a couple of bottles and moved to the bar to throw them out, passing the mirror. For a moment, I looked in the mirror. I almost missed it. Staring back at me was Luna's face - in so many ways similar to mine, but in really important ways, so different.

I stared, moving my face back and forth. The image of Luna moved with me. I opened my mouth.

And so did she.

I must have been hallucinating. I said "Hello," and the voice was mine. I smiled. Luna smiled back at me. Her lips moved.

"Wait."

That wasn't my voice. It was Luna's melodic sing songy voice. I watched her lips move.

"Come get me."

Tee

It was three days until we could use Luna again. Looking at her and knowing that it was Emmi inside her was crazy. She still looked so much like me, in a way. I'd come to think of Luna as my other self.

Meijo met us out in the Launch room. We planned to go out dancing before going back to a party. I wanted to show Meijo what we could really do.

And Bron was right, this body was stunning. I was wearing a beautiful body, a black trans girl. It had wild hair and perfect skin, covered all over in tattoos, fantastic natural breasts and a really pretty dick.

It was nowhere near close to the size of Savi's but It was a showstopper. It was about the size of Rik's, but feminine somehow. It was beautiful. It slid easily under me so I could tuck it away in the white shorts I was wearing.

I stepped lightly on Tee's model-like legs to kiss Meijo.

"Oh, wow."

"What do you think?"

"I still like your own body best, but that is pretty."

"I know, isn't it amazing?

Meijo kissed Luna's lips with Emmi inside. "How do YOU feel?"

"Tall and stacked." She pulled Luna's breasts out of the shirt and played with them. They really were remarkable.

"Ok, Miejo, check this out." I pulled Tee's shorts down and pulled out the perfect dick, letting it swing between my legs.

"Ha. That is amazing." He put his hand on it and petted it. It was responding quickly and it was an intense feeling. I'd worn strap-ons so many times, but this was so different.

Emmi looked at me, "isn't it wild?"

"Yes, jeez. I know what you mean. I just want to shove it in something."

Luna dropped her pants and made her way to the overstuffed couch. "Can you try it with me?"

I remembered that it was Emmi in there and that I was basically in the body of a goddess, too. I held the dick up in my hand and stepped over to her. I kicked off the shorts and climbed on between her open legs. She looked nice and wet and I remembered how it felt wearing that body. I knew how good it felt when that pussy was open and being filled up. I pulled at the thick piece of meat between my legs and Emmi pulled me down. She whispered. "It's me, Emmi. I want you so bad, Seka."

Hearing her say my name was the last little piece I needed to get fully erect. The cock was warm and hard in my hands and I placed the tip right at the opening of her cunt lips. Lifting my ass up, I slowly pressed it into the folds of her pussy. Emmi spread Luna's legs even wider, pulling them up over her head.

She was used to being flexible. In her hands, Luna was a contortionist, spreading her pussy open so wide that Tee's dick seemed to slip into it deeper and deeper before reaching bottom. She grabbed my shoulders and moaned in Luna's pretty melody of a voice. I remembered what it felt like for her.

But I didn't have any frame of reference for what this would feel like.

It just felt right. It felt like this was where this cock was supposed to be. I drove it home into the docking station and everything inside of her seemed to lock in like it was just a perfect fit. I was immersed. I was hypnotized.

I spread Tee's legs wide and pressed my thighs down on Emmi. She was touching my face, adoring me. I heard her whisper over and over, "Seka." and I knew she was imagining my face. That felt amazing.

She closed her eyes. I thought about Emmi's pussy, all pink and melting, warm and liquid, and how she could open it so wide like this. I put my hands behind me and let Tee's admittedly slight body weight drive my dick even deeper. I reach around and spread my ass for Miejo, pointing it directly at him behind us.

A few seconds later, I felt his hands on Tee's ass, massaging it, slipping his fingers into it. I started to move back and forth, rocking inside Emmi. She wrapped her arms around me and kept whispering. Suddenly, I hoped that Meijo was falling in love with her because that was something we could do together. We could fuck her and love her and take care of her together. As i thought that, I realized how badly I wanted that.

I whispered back at her, "Emmi, I want you so badly. I want you to exercise on my face every day."

She laughed and breathed in sharply. I let go of my ass as I felt Meijo's dick slide between Tee's asscheeks, invading the little hole. That felt so right, too. I realized that this body had a prostate as his prick rammed up against it, almost pushing me over the edge. I grit my teeth and grunted, trying not to cum. This was going to be impossible. As the tip of his dick flipped against my spot on the inside, the incredibly sensitive tip of my own rod was gently sucked by Luna's open cunt. I had never imagined anything like this and now all my effort was going into staying strong, keeping the rhythm, preventing myself from losing it all completely.

I closed my eyes. Looking anywhere, thinking anything, listening, smelling, just brought me closer to release. I had no idea this would be so hard.

Meijo fucked my ass softly, delicately, in rhythm with my movements fucking Emmi. I could hear him breathing behind me but I needed him not to say anything right now while his beautiful fucking dick was edging me like this. For a second it seemed like he was doing all the work, fucking both of us and the thought of that brought me too close.

I grunted and held my breath. My tits slapped against Luna's now as she raised her hands over her head. She leaned back and I could feel Luna's pussy cumming all over my dick, mixing with the pre-cum spilling out of me.

I felt so lucky to be in the middle of this as Meijo's cock exploded. He drove it deeper into me and rode me harder, pushing my own dick into Emmi. A white light flashed across my eyes as my whole body shivered and I poured my cum out into her, fucking myself on Meijo's rutting cock at the same time.

Emmi was whispering in Luna's pretty voice under me, thanking me for my cum, calling me by name, telling me how much she wanted to be fucked by me.

Loving me.

***

We were supposed to meet Rik and some friends at a club he chose. It was called "Orizaba" after a very tall mountain not too far away. It was broken into three parts, Pico was at the top. It was a beautiful, glass enclosed penthouse area that had a brilliant view of the entire city, Escalada, the middle area, was a massive dance area surrounded by bars with a big circular dance floor, and Subrísa, the basement, an anything-goes club area for explorers.

We started at the top, at Pico, with a light dinner. Rik, Eiko, Tanya and a few others met us and we sat around a long table.

The music was new and soft and Emmi and I wore see-through clothing to show off these new bodies. We doted on Meijo and showed the whole place what it looked like when a man had beautiful women all over him. It was so much fun and it amused Rik no end.

Rik looked a little more tense when we got down to Escalada, though, and I couldn't figure out why. He sat at the side bar while the rest of us were dancing. I split off and sat next to him.

"Do you not dance anymore, human?"

"I do. I did. Didn't you see?"

"Yeah, I'm just fucking with you. You ok?"

"Oh, yeah. Take a look." He pointed over to the bar and a familiar looking woman was laughing with the bartender. She was lighter skinned than Tee, with cornrows, in a black button down shirt.

"Is that…"

"Cerrone Michaels." Rik took a drink.

"So, that's not a coincidence, is it?"

"No. She owns this place. I don't know what I was expecting. Like if i saw her I'd figure it out."

"But nothing."

"Nope, nothing."

"So, what do you think she and I have in common?"

"I don't know. "

"You want her DNA, don't you?"

"I kind of do."

"You sneak. How do we get it?"

"She hasn't drunk anything since I've been watching."

"You want to see something sweet?"

"I do."

I waved over a woman standing not too far from Cerrone. She looked at me and walked over. I put on my best flirty Tee demeanor.

"Hello."

"Do I know you?"

"No, you do not. I hate to bug you. Is that Cerrone?"

"Oh, over there?"

"Yes. I love this place and I promised myself if i saw her I would buy her a drink."

"A drink, huh?"

"Is that stupid? I've just had soooo much fun here."

She looked at me, sizing up Tee. She looked down at the bar and my eyes followed her. Flipping over her hand she showed me a tattoo on her inner wrist.

It was the swoop and circle representing the Senza Dolore.

"You're going to behave yourself?" She smiled.

I smiled back. "Girl, I am so well behaved."

Rik turned around and I saw her tap Cerrone on the shoulder. She pointed to me and then Cerrone Micheals walked over, wiping her hands with a towel. She smiled.

"So, you want to buy me a drink?"

"Oh my god. I do."

"Have I seen you around here?"

"I've been really shy, but I'm really coming out and I owe it to your bar. Can I buy you a drink? Is that dumb?"

"No, it's not dumb. Let's do it. You are..." She extended her hand.

"I'm Tee Kaska. I can't believe I'm shaking your hand."

"What do you drink?" She smiled.

"I will literally drink with you anything you want.

She pulled out two shotglasses and a bottle and filled them with a rich rose colored liqueur. They were big shots, no lie.

"Ok. We make this here. Are you good?"

"I am so good. And I'm going to tip you so hard."

Her face opened up into a big smile as she lifted her glass. I lifted mine to mirror her.

And we both pounded them and slammed the glasses on the counter.

"Wow, I wasn't expecting that to be good. I thought you were going to mess me up." I laughed and grabbed her glass.

"Maybe next time, Tee Kaska."

"Thank you again for everything you do here. Imma party so hard tonight."

Cerrone Michaels walked away smiling, back to managing her club.

I moved closer to Rik and slid him the glass under the bar.

"You're fucking scary."

"You've never been afraid of me before."

"I'm seeing new sides of you, Tee Kaska."

"I'm seeing new stuff all the time. Like why do you think the Senza Dolore are protecting Cerrone Michaels?"

Rik looked at me and shook his head.

***

We headed down to Subrísa and watched. In the middle of the floor, a group of girls were dancing sexy together, topless. Near the far wall, two women stood completely nude, whipping and torturing a very happy looking man hanging from chains attached to the wall. And hanging above us, three woman with strap ons were on a floating platform, taking turns violating each other over and over.

There were men there, but the energy was strongly female, with women dominating each scene. Emmi grabbed Meijo's hand and pulled him over to a hammock hanging near the door. It was a very visible space.

Luna was wearing one of Emmi's signature short skirts with nothing underneath and as she pulled herself into the hammock you could see her pretty shaved pussy, darker than Emmi's own, glistening just a little in the club lights.

I watched as she pulled Meijo's face between her legs and let him suck on the pussy, his hands wrapped around the rope supports for the hammock. They rocked back and forth as he ate her out, with her head falling backward off the hammock.

I felt Tee's cock get hard the more I watched. Tanya pulled Eicko over to a matching hammock and put her red-tufted cunt into his mouth. He started sucking with abandon while she pet his head. She looked out into the room and took a deep breath.

The hammocks were far enough in the air that they provided a brilliant view to the happenings all across the room. Luna and Tanya's eyes surveyed the space, like twin queens on thrones, serviced by their court.

I grabbed Rik's hand and pulled him over to a big velvet chair with a view of the room as well. Rik read the room and knelt in front of the chair as i pulled off my top, letting Tee's breasts drink in the sweaty musk of the space. I slid my pants down and untucked the pretty dick between my legs, pushing it down so I could run it over his waiting face.

I was rock hard already, watching Luna wipe up her pussy with Meijo's face. And Tanya was suffocating Eicko now in her asshole, her red, raw cunthole dripping onto his face. It was so pretty to watch.

I sat down and pulled Rik's face toward me, sliding my thick, Black dick between his lips. He made his mouth wet and pulled it in, serving that rod so well. He licked the shaft and flicked his tongue over the tip. I lifted it up and put Tee's balls in his mouth, letting him wash them with his tongue. He tried to reach his tongue around behind them and suck at Tee's asshole so I lifted up and let him.

Rick had never sucked my ass before and I loved seeing his handsome face down there cleaning me all over. I thought about all the times I'd casually sucked his dick and sucked his cum and piss down my throat, waiting for more and it felt good to just sit back and let his mouth do all the work.

I put my hands behind my head and lifted Tee's legs up to the handrests, sliding down in the velvet seat and I felt really comfortable.

Rik sucked away at my core as I relaxed and listened to the music fill the room. I could tell he wanted my cum and I loved how much this body came, remembering how I'd filled up Luna's hole earlier, with wave after wave of hot salty cum. I put my hand on Rik's head and pet him. His hair was soft and curly like a baby lamb, dark and sexy and mine right now.

"Do you want my cum, baby?"

He nodded so fast, excited, entranced. I'd never seen Rik like this before, but he'd seen me, begging, wanting, hoping for him to fill my mouth and use me, to explode in me so that I could drink it all down.

"Are you sure?"

He sucked harder, pulling at my dick with his lips, trying so hard to coax it out of my dick, to feel the wash of it in the back of his throat. I wondered how Tee's cum tasted, if her swell of Jism would be thick and salty and powerful, filling up his mouth until he couldn't breathe.

I laughed a little and saw flashes across the insides of my eyes as I filled his mouth with wave after wave of affection, riding his face until the end of my orgasm.

***

When we got back, a lot of us slept in my den that night. I had gotten off with the Tee body about four times but I still wanted to just get up and try masturbating. Would it be like giving myself a handjob?

I grabbed a juice from the bar and stepped over to where Rik had set up his computer stuff. He had stayed awake, apparently, to analyze the DNA samples he had gotten. I looked at his screen. He had my DNA and Cerrone's up, along with the three LifeQuest bodies. It looked like he was marking off two separate areas in the bodies where a gene sequence was identical. One are, he'd shown me before, was mine.

The other, clearly, was Cerrone's. So the bodies were built from her, as well.

From both of us.

Somehow these things were composed of the DNA from multiple people and Cerrone and I were both donors. I clicked the area that represented Cerrone. It was just about as large as Mine.

When clicking back to the other part, I must have accidentally double clicked. It asked me for a password for Bronwell Carter.

This was still connected to Bron's computer.

I paused for a second and then, without thinking, typed it in.

"Natural"

A box popped up. It had a heading "Karyomorph" and showed a complex arrangement of my own DNA.

I clicked on Cerrone's portion.

A similar box popped up with the top heading "Geniploid," showing Cerrone's DNA arranged much the same way.

I did not know either of those words.

I turned to Rik, about to wake him up to ask when Emmi stepped up bchind me, startling me.

"Fuck. I'm sorry. I didn't know you were awake."

In Luna's melodic voice, she said, "You have to take me."

I smiled. I could go another round with Emmi. But something seemed off. It was almost like she was sleepwalking.

"Please take me. Seka."

It wasn't Emmi talking. I could see it now in her eyes. It was Luna.

"Please."

And she collapsed onto the floor.

Red

In Oregon, Senza Dolore had voted unanimously not to eject men from the state. Apparently the proposal had been floated by the opposition, pushing them to do something that would lose support.

And it backfired.

By not attempting to kick out men, they gained even more support from moderates, especially ones who liked their other policies, education initiatives, food programs and more. After less than a week, Senza Dolore was being seen as the common sense option.

And people in South California were watching.

***

After I'd woken up the Luna body, Emmi said she had no memory of talking to me. She figured she must have been sleepwalking. It was no big deal, she said, But she was still afraid to go to sleep.

We stayed up for hours just cuddling, hugging, kissing.

The Luna body was perfect, but I found myself missing Emmi's pale skin, pink parts and flat, seamless chest. I missed her smile and the way her voice started and stopped when we talked. The feelings were so real it almost made me believe her when she told me she missed my body, my face, my voice.

I almost believed it.

I felt Luna's weight on me when I woke up in the back bedroom. At some point in the night, she had climbed on top of me and put Tee's pretty cock inside of her. As the sun rose, I felt her warm and wet enveloping me. I had obviously fallen asleep inside of her. I didn't want to move and as I came to life, Tee's member grew inside her and I wrapped my arms around her.

I realized I was feeling close to Emmi and to Luna at the same time. I tried not to move and wake her up. I closed my eyes and thought.

I wondered if I could connect with the Tee body the way I did with Luna. Was there a part of her in here? I let myself really relax, breathing in and out on a natural rhythm. I tried to see inside this body, and find out if Tee was here. A part of me knew this was all fantasy, But I still looked deeper.

Before I knew it, there was a kind of redness behind my eyes. At first it was like the color that happens when you press your eyes shut too hard. Then it began to swirl and evolve. I could see space in it. The red opened up in front of me.

It looked raw and meaty, but inviting. In a way, I was reminded of the view I got of Tanya's pussy last night. She was ruddy and looked always on the verge of sunburn. Was her skin irritated or just alive, fresh, open?

Her cunt was rosy and the lips thick and full. And the red hair that framed her face grew in thickly under her arms and below her belly, making her feel even more immediate and physical. I realized that I processed her as a body. As a beautiful and primal body, the way I was seeing Tee now.

Tee was sitting across from me now cross legged, Her skin was dark and sleek, reflected unseen fires with its slick highlights. Behind her was an endless expanse of night, that brief moment when the world goes red.

I looked down, in this place, and saw my own body. I was naked as well, my skin wet with sweat. I was round, thick, and my breasts hung in a way on my chest that I only now saw as powerful, imperious.

My belly jutted out in front of me on top of the thickness of my own legs, sitting cross legged. I felt like fertility, like sculpture. This was the first time in my mind that my own body had appeared as an agent of something other than aversion, dislike, even disgust. My olive skin danced with the same red flickering motion as the rest of the scene. As Tee.

Tee and I were the same. We were made of the same thing. And we were a pantheon. I looked to my right and saw Luna's body, smiling, eyes closed, but seemingly aware. Her perfect breasts were rising and falling slowly. She seemed to validate our elevation. She was a goddess and so were we. We were a triumvirate. Tee looked at me and her beautiful pillow-like lips moved.

"Distance doesn't matter."

I suddenly understood.

The red night shifted and opened up and, to my left, I saw Savi's body sitting there, kneeling with his hands in his lap. He was only slightly darker than me and Luna and his skin seemed more alive now, as though the energy of the red were playing across its surface. I wondered where the fire was, the fire reflecting on all of us, but I didn't expect to see it.

I had only seen Savi as a body, as a cock, as a tool, muscles, physicality. Here, in the red, I saw the kindness on his face. I saw his real power. His chest was rising and falling slowly and it was in rhythm with ours. I felt in my womb now, like I had birthed gods. It made me feel warm inside, wet, powerful. I felt like shouting.

I looked down and I could see blood dripping from me. It was as if I had just begun to menstruate. I put my fingers between my legs. The blood was dark and slick and reflected the shifting light of the crimson world around me. It seemed to go on forever, as though each drop were an ocean.

Each drop a world.

Savi opened his eyes to look at me and I could see them, white. His pupils were milky and soft, as though he couldn't see. I could feel for a moment what he felt.

Afraid. Alone.

My heart opened up to him. There was something like love coupled with the duty of creation. My body tried to make it all so simple. We were growing things, evolving. And we needed things.

We needed.

An instinct hit me. I crawled over to where he sat and held his head. He leaned into me as I wiped the blood in my fingers across his eyes like warpaint. I leaned in and kissed him, realizing that, for all the play, I don't think I had actually kissed his lips before.

As I pulled back I saw his eyes. They were bright and clear, dark, endless, nearly black. They glistened now as his eyes welled up. He could see. He made a motion to stand up.

And his body faded

I reached inside me and covered my hand with the blood, pressing it against Tee's face. She closed her eyes, opening them clear and deep and piercing. She smiled and started to get up. I felt a slight brush of wind as she, too, faded away.

Crawling to Luna, I cradled her head, Anointing her eyes with the blood from between my legs. I kissed her. I felt her lips open and kiss me back, her hand moving to the back of my head. I leaned into it and let go, even as the room shifted and changed around me. The rich warmth of the red faded away to the crisp darkness of the back bedroom where Luna's body was moving back and forth on my cock,

I don't know how long that had been going on, while I was in my vision, but it felt like I was near cumming.

Luna's body was sleek and wet and it felt like we'd been connected forever, even while, at the same time, the pressure of her cunt on the meat between my legs was new, novel, exciting.

"Fill me up, Seka." Emmi said as she rode me, slamming her cunt down hard on Tee's midsection. I managed to say her name at least twice before the torrent of cum came pouring out of me, seeping into her. Emmi spread her legs wide and pulled me closer, her hands down by my ass. I laid my hands over her eyes and the red warpaint played across her face,

It wasn't until we had lain there for a while that we noticed that we were covered all over in menstrual blood.

Luna's period had started.

***

Rik and Eiko had gone to work, but we found Meijo and Tanya naked in the pit, wrapped up in each other, still asleep, his face between her legs as she lay on the couch. I gave her belly a quick kiss and then kissed his face.

As I knelt over him his eyes opened and he smiled at me, opening his mouth for Tee's kiss. I slid in next to him.

He held me close and we rocked back and forth. I was still on fire from my vision, still rubbery and relaxed from Emmi, still high from the last couple of weeks of exploration and release, still awash with feelings from everything altogether. But I was sane, and things made sense.

I whispered in his ear and hugged him close.

"I think I'm ready now."

***

Bron told us that, while the bodies were designed not to menstruate, it wasn't unheard of. And, most likely the recent trauma from the pulse gun had just kickstarted her system.

But she was healthy. The body was one of the healthiest ones he'd ever seen.

He gave me his card with his personal number on it. And Emmi and I came back home in our own bodies.

The cabdriver ignored me. Then he called Emmi "sir," without bothering to really look behind him. I wished we'd taken a standing monocab, but my legs didn't feel up to it.

I felt soft today, just as myself. I was an open nerve.

Meijo and Tanya were cleaning up. He didn't believe in the maid, even though he'd seen countless examples of her machinations all over the house. I think he may have thought I was inventing her, cleaning up myself when he wasn't looking. I thought that was hilarious. My own boyfriend doesn't believe in the maid.

He was my boyfriend.

Emmi and I took his hand and dragged him to superbed. Tanya came along, wiping her hand in a towel as she flopped into an overstuffed chair near the bed to watch. She smiled at me. She leaned back in the chair in her black panties and I wasn't afraid to have an observer.

I wasn't afraid of anything.

I pushed Meijo down and started kissing him with my own lips and it felt wonderful. I licked at his face and I forgot all about everything else. I saw Emmi pulling his shorts down as he started sliding my shirt off over my head. He flicked off my bra and dove into my breasts, sucking the tips as Emmi licked the tip of his dick.

We stayed like that for a while, with his hard cock growing under the ministrations of her mouth and his hands all over my tits. I felt free, more free than I had in a long time.

I pulled my pants down and slid out of my black underwear.

I shivered as Meijo put his hand on my belly, but then the red filled my mind, and I felt it. I was a goddess in the red. I was the fertility icon that drew hands, eyes, everything. I was creator.

I let my legs fall to the sides and Emmi slid in between them and kissed my pussy, slowly at first, then with more intensity. I'd never had someone's face between my own legs in my own body and it felt impossibly intimate. All I could think about was what I tasted like, what could be wrong with me.

Meijo kissed his way down my body and licked my belly, his tongue tracing my bellybutton. He turned me over and I rolled onto Emmi's head, as she sucked at my clit and open pussy. Meijo kissed his way down my cheeks, putting his face in my asshole and tonguing me slowly, methodically. Two mouths, devouring me. It was wonderful.

I got up the nerve to press my pussy into Emmi's face as she licked harder, trying to get her lips and tongue as far into me as she could. And Meijo did the same with my ass, pulling the cheeks apart and digging his tongue into my ass, becoming more and more lost in me.

I never thought I could be someone that people could GET lost in as I rocked back and forth. My ass was wet and open and I could feel Meijo's face inside me. I started rubbing myself harder against Emmi, feeling the connection and the slick motion on my clit. I could feel myself beginning to cum and I initially wanted to apologize for the waves of cum that started dripping out of me until I heard her sucking harder, lapping it up.

She was happy.

I knew I was ready.

As I rolled over, Emmi placed her mouth on my tit, holding me tight around the ass. My legs were open as Meijo climbed on top of me. He laid his hand against my cheek and whispered, "Are you ok?"

I nodded and wrapped my left arm around him, placing my hand on his ass.

I held Emmi's hand tightly and pulled Meijo into my waiting pussy. I stared up at the skylight. It was beginning to rain, and it made it feel good, safe, to be here, to be inside.

"Is this all right?"

I nodded furiously. "Please. Please. It's good."

It felt better than I could have imagined. It felt primal and immediate and so much stronger in my own body, Meijo's cock moved back and forth inside me and I instantly felt like exploding again. I felt the root of him rubbing against my clit and it made me feel soft and warm and it pulled me into him. Electricity bounced across my skin. II breathed into his neck as I gripped Emmi's hand. She leaned over and kissed my breast and I was enveloped, covered, little, inside a great body made up of the three of us.

His weight wasn't much on top of me but I reveled in it, I wanted it. I wanted to be crushed, pressed down. I wished that both of them were on top of me, flattening me.

How could feeling crushed feel so liberating?

"Damn." Meijo panted. I could tell Meijo was trying not to cum. The sound of him trying put me over the top. Cum poured out of me now, and I could hear how wet my pussy was as he violated it, pressing himself into it. My legs spread wider and my head lolled back, as he slid in even deeper. I wanted him to fall all the way in, to get lost in me, to fill me with his whole self. All friction had been replaced with wet, fluid compromise as our bodies worked together like one organ.

My cunt was so hungry now, wanting, open and waiting for him to let go, I whispered in his ear,

"C'mon, fill me up. Please. I want it."

I loved the fact that he had to try to hold back. He was inside me and it was powerful enough that he had to try.

"You can let go. You can cum. It's ok, baby." I moaned louder, hoping Tanya was masturbating to this.

I thought about her being the last one he fucked and wondered if he came in her like this.

He let out a cry and let go inside of me. A wave of cum poured into my own pussy for the first time. I pet his head and waited, glacing at Tanya. She was fingering herself in the chair, watching as Emmi held us both. Meijo kept cumming, like a fountain hose turning off and on, and it felt not rushed by long, so long.

But never long enough. The rain came down overhead and I felt it, warm and wet.

Never long enough.

***

Meijo fell asleep on the superbed. I left him there and joined Emmi and Tanya in the pit for a massive glass of wine.

Emmi knelt in front of me, making a big deal out of licking all of Meijo's cum out of me while Tanya sat next to me, fascinated. The rain had gotten more dense, and it made us feel more cradled here in the house. All the skylights were passing tiny raindrop sounds from room to room, like little footsteps.

"So, the first time in your own body?"

"The very first time."

"Damn." Tanya shared that she was mostly into girls and that Meijo was only the second man she's had penetrative sex with and that was just last night. That somehow made me feel less like an anomaly and more normal. I shared with her my aversion to sex in my own body, a mental block I seem to have overcome tonight.

"How do you feel?"

"I feel more like a rational person. I'm not driven by bizarre mental blocks I can't trace. I was so driven by this big mysterious past event and now I'm free to not care."

"To not give a shit."

"Yeah. like it doesn't matter."

Emmi kissed her way up my body and I was glad, in a way, she was done. Too much more of that and it would have sucked me in again. I handed her a glass."

Tanya lifted her glass, "I'm glad I found all you perverts. I was starting to lose hope that there were more people like me." She shook her hair and for a brief moment, it looked like her head was on fire.

"To us," Emmi and I toasted. Tanya was right. In this weird world that looked like it just barely might survive the constant explosions of the past, everything was so delicate and on-the-edge. Somehow, we'd fallen into a group of people who were free, able to just let go. And we could make our own little thing.

Emmi gave me a kiss, "I'm going to go check on the dude."

I grabbed her and kissed her longer. "Give him that," and she laughed. She had been so bouncy since she had tried the Savi body. It's like she realized how much fun it was for her to be small. She ran back to the bedroom. I looked down and tried to remember where I'd left my robe.

It's important that people recognize this chain of events, I think.

I walked into the hallway to find my robe and stopped. Right in front of me was Savi. He was breathing heavily and carrying a large bag over his shoulder. He was drenched, water pouring off of him from the rain.

"You're here." He said, moving forward.

I took a step. Looking in his eyes I could see it.

There was no one piloting the body. No one was inside. It was just him.

"Savi?" I whispered.

"It's me. You have to help me."

He dropped the bag and fell onto his knees. He looked exhausted. He tipped over and fell onto the ground.

I tried to lift him but he was too heavy. The body was dense and immobile.

Then, I heard a scream.

Stepping back into the den, I saw Tanya coming from the bedroom. She looked terrified,

"Come here, quickly."

Change

According to the Kunai Notebooks, the history of transgender surgery can be traced back to 1500 BC in Ancient Egypt. Trangender procedures have been a topic of concern for human beings since the beginning of recorded history, apparently. There were transgender operations in ancient Rome and even efforts to mediate and change gender in prehistoric Greece.

We can only assume that there have always been transgender people. Nothing we see in evidence suggests it is a modern preoccupation or temporary concern. Very in-depth reports of Vaginoplasty from the 2nd century, in fact, guided much of what people moving forward knew about the shape and form of the vagina.

What men knew.

But, the modern period of Gender-affirming surgical care probably began in the 1920s in Berlin, Germany at the Institute for Sexual Research, run by doctor Magnus Hirschfeld. At the time, it was vital for them to stay out of sight of the growing Nazi party, which had unilaterally made research into this field illegal, as most far right wing authoritarian regimes did throughout history.

Controlling gender on the state level is very important for them.

During the great loss, many transgender people found themselves going underground again. There was a virtual hard stop on all ongoing research.

Much of the knowledge that had been accumulated in regards to gender affirming surgical care had been lost, as well as research into DNA reconstruction, stem cells, and other methods of achieving similar outcomes.

Today, it seemed like we were learning all over again. And much of the transgender care available had been simply cosmetic, such as Tee's body. The hope was that truly convincing vaginoplasty and penile implant operations were just decades away, and we all had friends who were waiting, hoping.

Which is why what I saw in the bedroom was so completely foreign to me, unbelievable in every way.

Meijo was panicking, while Emmi was holding him, trying to calm him. Immediately, something seemed different about him. He was still naked, wrapped in covers, and at first glance he looked thinner, his face more refined. He looked more clean shaven than I'd ever seen him, and his hair seemed to be falling differently around his face. I approached him and he yelled out, stopping me in my tracks. He'd never pushed me away before and it made my heart sink. The way that Emmi was coddling him made me feel like he was sick, like something horrible was wrong. But he appeared healthy. He kicked the covers away and I could see it. None of it made any sense. His chest, normally flat with a slight range of black hair, was now completely smooth. And two perfect breasts had sprouted there. As first I thought it was some trick of the light until He dug his face into Emmi's arms and the rest of the covers fell off.

I saw what it was that made him scream. Between his legs, covered minimally with a smattering of black hair was an unexpected, but beautiful, flawless woman's pussy.

It was Meijo's pussy.

**

In the Den, Savi was drenched, soaked to the bone. He seemed traumatized and lost, but he was open, talkative. Unlike Miejo who couldn't even look at me. Tanya and I went back and forth, alternating rooms.

Savi seemed lucid, aware, but quiet. He had a memory of being with us, of spending time with us, as Host to Emmi. But he said he was trapped during that time, just a small mind packed away in the back, waiting. He said he felt like he was made of little pieces of us and other people.

But he could tell I was different. Something about what had happened in the red space had freed him. And without thinking, he had broken out of LifeQuest and come here, the only place he could imagine going. He injected the handler with a sedative that had to be counteracted. He had only brought him with as insurance, in case he was stopped. He would stay sleeping in the bag until he injected him again. Without looking in the bag, I knew who it was.

If I'm struggling through this it's because it's all hard to process all at once. And I need you to be up to speed for what happens next. Again, if you have a problem with this, maybe you shouldn't be reading my journal.

Because it only gets worse.

***

Savi and I stepped into the bedroom where Emmi and Meijo were holding each other, crying. My heart dropped out of my chest. To see them there so hurt because of me was killing me. Meijo looked up and stared at me for a second.

Since he had changed, this was the first time he looked me in the eye.

He reached his hand out for me to come closer.

I started to cry and I ran to the bed and held him.

He felt different. His shape, his skin. He was different. But it was Meijo and everything I loved was still there. I held onto him as Emmi hugged us both. She motioned to Savi to come join us.

He knelt at the side of the bed and looked at Emmi. He was made of minds, different people, pulled together, residue of the people who had been inside that body people who had used it. And that included Emmi.

But there was something else there. And I could feel it now. It was a kind of an affinity, There was something of me in him.

And something else.

There was something that belonged in the red space. Something native to there. It was a kind of beauty, a kind of perfection.

Savi touched Emmi's face, as the pieces in him connected with her. Meijo drew me in and wrapped his new body around me. He was still crying. I held him and we rocked back and forth. He put his hands under my robe and pulled me closer. Something about the size of me, my curves, it was calming to him. I kissed him and his lips felt like a woman's. I realized that this was really happening.

He put his hand on mine and put it between his legs. I felt his pussy for the first time. It was warm and soft and wet and I explored it with my hand as I started to kiss him. His mouth opened under mine and we were kissing so deeply through tears, touching each other all over. I gingerly placed a finger inside him and he pulled my hand deeper, closer.

I couldn't believe he wanted me to touch him. I tried to burrow into him. This seemed more about healing than anything and I understood that. All of it was so bizarre and it just made no sense.

None of it did.

Emmi and Savi seemed connected, almost like they found each other, like he found someone he was supposed to be with. Between that and his connection with me, he belonged here, too, and Meijo accepted that. The last time he'd seen that body, Emmi was inside it.

And they had so many connections.

It was warm in there and I realized that this was the most people that had ever been in superbed at the same time. I let Meijo kiss me.

He seemed to want to be in charge of that part of our connection, moving his lips with purpose. And I just wanted it. I wanted to know he was ok. He pulled at me like he was afraid I would disappear or leave and that was so much of what I needed after feeling pushed away, like I had hurt him.

He was the center of our world now and Emmi leaned in and began to kiss his breasts. They were average sized and perfectly round and so smooth that it was impossible to believe there was hair there just a few hours ago. His nipples were dark and brown and popped up from his chest in a way that invited the tongue.

HIs nipples made it clear, through morphology, that they were made to be sucked on, made to fit the mouth as puzzle pieces that reflected the history of bodies and the story of birth, procreation, passion.

Like the body high that I felt in the red space where every part of the flesh we all wore was optimized in some great organic machine made of history and evolution, where each piece of us was the inevitable conclusion to a dance built with billions of bodily connections, through intercourse and birth and death as far back as you could see.

I welcomed his fingers inside me and spread my legs so he could find my spot, the places in me that responded to him. These aren't things I was used to doing while in my own body and, while I considered what I had done, what this body may have done to him, I also realized that he had earned, through years of his affection and grace and effulgence, a kind of lack of fear from me.

It would have been silly for me to ever be afraid of him. It would have hurt my heart right now to pull back, to close myself off to him, especially when it was he that I wanted so badly.

I didn't expect this, but soon I felt the warmth of a liquid wave pouring out of me.

I felt the wetness beneath me spreading and becoming a hole, a figurative hole, that we could all fall in and be lost.

Emmi had dropped her robe, too, and pulled off Savi's shirt. He played with her pussy now as he helped her explore Meijo's new body. Meijo lifted his ass from the bed and spread his legs, his hand firmly inside me, pulling me closer. Savi kissed his belly and let his tongue run lower, licking at him and kissing his mound before diving in and anchoring his face on Meijo's new cunt.

I was equal parts turned on by my closeness to Meijo and this novelty of being able to connect with him in this new way, but also terrified at the change and what I had a part in, what I had done. At the same time, we were all exhausted. There was an aura in the warm wetness of the room that this was a womb and we were pre-language, pre-birth, bodies asleep but waking up for the first time.

Savi moved up his body and they kissed. With his other hand, Meijo pulled out Savi's cock and ran his fingers over it. Strangely, as we'd been getting to know him as a person, and not just a body, his dick seemed more reasonable, more approachable. It didn't seem impossibly large now, but something human and desirable.

I put my hand on his dick, alongside Meijo's and felt it getting harder, throbbing with the energy of the room. I kissed Meijo's neck, pulling him closer as he tried to drag me toward him by my pussy, digging his hand into it, nails and all.

I loved the feeling. His fingers were a little sharp, thin, hard, like claws pulling at me. I wanted it to hurt, to feel more aggressive and mean. I wanted to feel the need in it as he dragged my cunt to him for warmth, for solace, for anything. My pussy pulsed with wanting to be used for something, no matter how primal and cruel. I realized I wanted to offer him my open raw hole for any purpose and just wanted it to be used to satisfy him.

I placed the tip of Savi's dick in Meijo's new cunt, aiming it toward the sleek entryway, making a straight line for Savi to push it inside.

He sucked on Savi's tongue and moaned, louder now. His voice was lighter, softer, even higher as he begged for it.

"Fuck, do it. Fuck me."

I bit at his neck and opened my cunt to him as wide as I could while helping Savi slide his prick deep Into Meijo's waiting hole. As big as it was, his wet pink pussy seemed to suck every inch of it in as fast as I could push it, Bathing it with his slick juices.

Meijo groaned and lowered his head, leaning to his right to take in Emmi's tongue. He held tight onto the front of my cunt, squeezing his hand tight as it wrapped around my clit and lips. I felt like i couldn't move away and I loved the feeling- being immobilized by his hand treating my hole like a mountain nook, holding on tight as he climbed, afraid to fall.

Savi pulled back and dove in deeper, pushing his fuck into Meijo, smashing his ass into the bed with every downstroke. We all moved together as one organism, connected. Meijo was clinging to Emmi's pussy, and I hoped that she felt what I did, that same need, that same desire to never let go, his mountain-climber tenacity pulling us toward his center where Savi was filling this new hole with his massive body, pushing himself into Meijo like he wanted to crawl inside and live there.

Savi moved harder and faster now, sensing that Meijo was ready, that his new cunt was prepared to explode. He pumped himself into him, his own orgasm coming now, building overflowing the gates of reason with waves of slick white ocean, brine from deep inside him.

Savi moved harder, faster now, sensing that Meijo was ready, that his new cunt was prepared to explode. He pumped himself into him, his own orgasm coming now, overflowing the gates of reason with waves of slick, white ocean, brine from deep inside him. The two of them pressed tight, bound by the deep sweat across their bellies, cumming while Savi hunched over him, hands wrapped in his slight black hair, mouths open and connected like holes through rock, grown together by erosion, becoming seamless.

Becoming timeless.

***

Rik had gotten here and Emmi and Savi were in the den with him now, trying to figure out what to do next. I wanted to talk to Meijo if I could and now he seemed open to it. We leaned back into the bed together.

"Well, I think we have a better idea of what happened with that Mika person now. This, I understand less" he pointed to the den and Savi.

"It's all crazy, though, isn't it?" I shook my head. "I made him biologically female just by having sex with him? We were twelve years old. How were we having sex? And how did I do it?"

"Is it part of this biological connection you have?"

"I don't think so. I mean, I think we all kind of have a connection through the red space. I think it's just the way that bodies are connected here in the world."

"I've never experienced anything like it. And I've clearly never experienced anything like this."

"Are you ok?"

"I think part of me thought having sex again might reverse it? But part of me is ok with it. Part of me is surprisingly ok with it, actually. I don't feel... wrong." He ran his hand through his hair. How was it that even his hair laid differently? In his biologically male body, it seemed maybe a little long, a bit wild and unkempt, maybe. Framing this new more feminine face, it just looked like his, like it was a woman's hair.

"You are beautiful, I mean, both ways, you are."

"If I think about it, I panic. If I imagine the future, try to figure out what I'm going to be, I panic."

I held him and my heart started racing. His voice dropped.

"Do you think it's reversible?"

This was the question I was afraid of. I just didn't know. And if it weren't would he hate me?

"We can try. I don't know anything about this."

"Do you think he does?"

I was afraid of this, too. We would have to get out of bed. "Let's find out."

***

Meijo hugged Rik and Tanya at the bar. He had pulled himself into a pair of his shorts and a baggy shirt. They didn't hide the obvious truth that his body was feminie now. If anything, they amplified what a pretty one he was, I thought, while staring at him.

"So, this is something that really happens," Rik started.

"Apparently. I turn male bodies into female ones by having sex with them."

Tanya stepped up, "Ok, not to be nit picky, but we don't really even know that for sure yet. We have two possible situations. In one, with that Mika person, you were very young. How were you having sex? In this case, we've all been so involved, doing so much, how do we know it was you that did it."

"That's true," Emmi jumped in, "The Savi Body, the Tee body, Rick, even Eiko all had sex with Meijo, topping him."

Rik raised his hand, "And I've had sex with another guy at that second party. He's still male."

Savi stood up full height, "I feel, like, remembering, that this body has had sex with men before and they haven't become women."

"So, It's probably me."

Rik nodded, "It is probably you."

"I ruin people's lives." I sat down.

"No, you have a very strange gift, but it's not about ruining lives." She went over to Rik's computer. "So we did a search for the term that you found."

I had told Tanya and Rik in the morning that i had, through complex mental gymnastics and skill, broken Bron's password and found how my DNA was described, "So, yes, Karyomorph. It just means the chromosomal makeup of someone with a certain form."

Rik stepped over, "That was one definition, the first one. Here is another one." He pointed to the screen.

I saw what he was pointing to. My legs almost gave out.

"No fucking way."

"Yep," Tanya affirmed.

Emmi moved over to the computer and read, "Any substance or organism capable of changing the Karyotype for another organism." She looked at me, "That is literally insane."

"How believable is this?" The net had fallen into complete disrepair during the great loss and virtually nothing you found on it was very believable. Over the last 50 years a lot of work had been done to make it something usable again, but there was still a lot that was just rumor, just conjecture or misdirection."

"So, here we go."

I looked up at Tanya, my shoulders sagged in relief. I appreciated her so much for making this into a simple, clinical thing.

"You're just a kid. Something happens where the boy next door plays with you, He changes into a biological female, LifeQuest somehow finds out, makes the whole thing go away, removes your memory and gives you both a lifelong trust fund so you would go looking for any answers."

Meijo raised his head, "Fuck."

Rick picked up, "They, they use what they learn from you to start this business."

"And you think the same thing happened to Cerrone Michale and the other people with trust funds?"

"I don't know. But someone might," Rik finished.

In the middle of the room was the bag that Savi had brought.

Savi looked around at us. "It might be time to wake him up."

Bron

"He's still going." Rik stood in the doorway watching Bron eat.

"He really does put it down." Emmi looked over at Savi, "How long was he asleep?

Savi unfolded his arms. Leaning up against the wall with his arms folded over his chest he looked like a championship wrestler. He was a big man. "I guess like a day and a half? I injected him and then kept him in a closet until I could get out."

"And then we have to get Tee and Luna out as fast as we can." Meijo seemed to be making himself small, recessive, pulling back. It hurt my heart to see.

Bron sat at the table, deftly eating a giant breakfast sausage. He bit on it in a way that made me cringe a tiny bit.

"Reason number two we need him." I mean, it could be easy.

"Do you guys just never wear clothes anymore? I mean, I'm not complaining, but…" Rik nodded at me and Emmi. We were still in robes, half open in front, naked underneath. Just a few months ago, I would have never walked around like this. But so much had happened since then.

A universe of things had happened.

"Weirdly enough, he seems more receptive to answering questions when we're like this. I figured I'd milk it for all it's worth."

"You know, I can hear you all." Bron was at the table, pulling two more pieces of french toast onto a plate. This was becoming the infinite breakfast.

"Is there anything else you want to eat?" I moved over to the table and leaned in.

He winked at me, "No, Imma finish what's here and we can discuss it. I know you have a lot of food here."

I sighed. "Can you talk while you eat?" I asked. I wasn't sure how much time we had.

"I cannot." He smiled up at me with that ruddy red face.

I reached over and pulled Meijo over. "Ok, starshine. This is my boyfriend. Do you remember him?"

Bron looked at us like I was nuts. Meijo lifted his shirt and showed off his tits. Bron spit a little on the table.

"No. I would remember those."

"Well, he was a male, now, after sex with me, he is female. Because I'm a Karyomrph?" I looked at his face to see some kind of recognition.

Suddenly, he broke out laughing, "Not fucking possible. Didn't happen."

"I'm a karyomorph?"

He shook his head and shrugged.

"The word is on your own computer. Your password. Natural? It says I'm a Karyomorph, my DNA, and that some of the other DNA comes from someone else, she is a geniploid? What is that?"

"I really don't know. I told you, I'm in the zoetics group. I don't access half the things I could."

He shoved some french toast in his mouth, "A lot of stuff I don't want to know. Hell, I forgot all this already. I'm forgetting shit while you're talking."

Tanya whispered to me, "Do you think he's telling the truth?"

I really had no idea. I shrugged. I can't believe this was a dead end. I looked at Savi.

"Ok. We need to rescue the Tee and Luna bodies."

"Rescue?" He looked at me. "I don't know what you did with that one," he waved a fork at Savi.

"He is... He sort of gained sentience. And we think those two bodies have, too."

"Well, fuck me. You are a superhero. So, let me encapsulate what we have learned. In contact with your immortal pussy, boys become girls and empty bodies spring to life."

"He's a dick." Tanya stole a piece of French Toast.

"I am." Bron smiled at me. "But I can help you get those bodies. If you really want them."

"How can you help?" I sat down across from him. I could see him looking at my tits through the robe and I opened it up a little. Because why the fuck not if it worked?

"I'm already holding those bodies for you. I can show you where to go and give you my access card. Then you just have to carry them out. Or you can wave your magic pussy and they can skip out with you. "

"You can do that?" I looked up at Emmi.

"I can. And then you do your big rescue, I finish eating. I report the card stolen and go back to work after taking a sick day to go shopping with the 20,000 dollars you give me."

This sounded easier than I even thought.

"Sold." I shot up and clapped my hands. "This is going to work." I looked over at Rik and he nodded.

"Ok, I'm in. Slavery is bad. Let's rescue some bodies."

"Absolutely," Emmi followed up.

Tanya looked at me, "Do you trust him?"

"What's not to trust? You kidnapped me, I'm helping you. 20,000 dollars and one more little thing and you go on with your life."

Meijo looked up over at Bron, "What more little thing?"

Bron shoveled another forkfull of food in his face and pointed the fork at me, "She has sex with me."

"Shit." Rik turned around, "This guy's full of shit."

"With me? Like this? In my body?"

"Yes, you know why. You know." He kept on eating. That was probably the least sexy part of this. He just kept right on eating."

Tanya stepped up, "There are a bunch of women here. Would you want to have sex with me instead?"

"You're hot, but you look more like one of those bodies," He wasn't wrong. Tanya was really very conventionally attractive. She and Rik could have been on slabs down at LifeQuest and people would pay. I put that thought out of my head.

Emmi let her robe drop. "I'm actually really good in bed. And I like anal a lot." She winked at him. Something about Emmi offering herself up for me made my heart melt. This was all so crazy.

Someone wanted to have sex with me this badly. So badly that they were just a total prick about it. "No, you're cute and I'll take some, but this little dance with me and her has been going on for a while now. This is where our deals have been headed, right?" He looked at my face for any sign that I wanted to.

I did not.

"First of all, are you nuts? Karyomorph? I literally change people's chromosomal makeup by having sex with them."

He sputtered, "Oh, you were serious? Oh my god, you really want me to believe that?"

"I showed you my boyfriend?"

"Oh, her, she's cute. She's like one of those LifeQuest user bodies, too. Hot, but regular." He looked over at Meijo, "No offense."

"Um. None taken?" Meijo tried his best to process any of that. He curled up his mouth at me to show confusion. Hot but Regular.

I was confused, too.

I grabbed Emmi and Meijo's hands and moved out into the hallway.

"Ok, you two. Am I doing this?"

"I tried, but, honestly, I didn't want to, either."

Meijo smiled, "And she famously does anal."

She kissed him on the nose, "Do you want some?"

"It's not so much about not wanting to. None of us really want to. But what if he changes into a biological woman?"

Meijo looked up, "He will be probably 50% more tolerable."

"True." Emmi held up her finger.

"Ok, I don't deny that at all, but what the fuck. Can I just be femming up the whole city, one at a time?"

Meijo cocked his head and made his hands into an explosion, "Magic pussy."

"He knows the risks. You told him at least three times." Emmi held up three fingers now.

Meijo considered, "is it your fault he doesn't believe you?"

"I should make him believe me."

Emmi started, "So, worst case, he has a pussy later on today."

"What if he decides to shoot himself, too?"

"That's not on you." Emmi shot back.

"Yeah. I mean, I'm in a bit of a haze and kind of freaked out, but I'm not shooting the place up."

"Because you're the most rational person in the world."

"It's kind of hot," Emmi interjected.

"You want me to be reasonable for you?" He slipped his arm around Emmi.

"Be logical for us, baby." Emmi kissed him and grabbed his crotch and he hugged us both. I put my head in his neck. This was normal. This was so normal. This, I wanted.

I didn't want any part of Bron.

Meijo kissed me on the lips. "We have to get Tee and Luna. If you saw them come to life in the red space, too, we have no choice. We can't leave them there. In fact, if you can wake up these bodies, do we have the right to leave any of them there?" Meijo's breath was warm against my face. It felt like him. No matter what else had changed.

"So I'm fucking him?"

"Can we make this easier for you?" Emmi kissed me.

"Can you cut my head off?"

***

I'm not going to go into detail with my experience having sex with Bron. Why? Because it just wasn't that much fun. I didn't let him cum in me and I think I probably laid there a little more than I ever have. It's called "Starfishing." Look it up.

Seriously, can you imagine me being laid back about sex? Usually I'm up and randy trying to suck every body fluid you have out of your body. Hell, I thought about Emmi kicking my cunt until it almost fell off in that launch room at lifequest and it was like a waterfall. All I wanted was for her to stick her entire foot up inside me, boots and all. I thought about all the times I'd kneeled down, waiting for Meijo to piss in my mouth, realizing that I hadn't done that yet with his new body and wishing I could just jump up and go do that.

Right now.

So many things I hadn't done with him yet. Every one sounded like the go-to thing to do today.

Instead, I was staring at the ceiling while Bron moved back and forth on top of me, shoving his cock in me abstractly.

Oh, he was working pretty hard at it. I was just elsewhere.

Here are the things that WERE kind of hot. Technically, this was my first foray into prostitution. Someone wanted to fuck me so badly that they are giving us stuff we need in exchange.

This part was not un hot. But here is the thing that was more hot. I'm only telling this part to my journal. If you want to keep reading, that's on you.

So fuck you if you get all judgy and shit.

These people who were MY people, Meijo, Emmi, Rik, Tanya, even Savi. All of them had basically had free rights to my body. They could do what they wanted and they, at times, had. They were my people. They all had a goal, an agenda, and in order to get it, they had to sacrifice me, just for an hour or two, to be used and violated. So they gave me over and I did my job.

Meijo telling me why I needed to do this made it hot. Emmi, all of them. This is what I had to keep thinking. And I made it through the event as a sort of sacred temple whore, whose holy duty was outlined by the people she loved, so she opened her garment and did her fucking job.

Which was literally fucking. As a job.

***

"You have his card?" I asked Rik plopping myself down into the Pit.

"Well, if it isn't the little temple whore."

"How did you know about that?"

"You were saying it to yourself when you went in there." Meijo shifted toward me and Emmi followed."

"O, jeez, really?" I hadn't realized I said it out loud. That was badass.

"And, yes, I do. And his codes." Rik held up the pass. "Is dude in there resting?"

"He is." I shot back. "I can't say I put my back in it. And before you ask, no, he has no weapons."

Maijo kissed me, "Are we all your pimps now?"

"Oh, please. Please be my pimps. I may need you two to just piss all over me."

Emmi laughed, "done."

"I want to try joining you in the Red space."

"Oh, yeah? I turned to Tanya.

Savi jumped in, "We were talking about it."

"What if we could free all the bodies in there?"

"I'm game, absolutely."

"I was thinking about that," Rik stood up and grabbed his computer. "This is something you can do, and Savi can do it, too, right? The bodies you saw in there. Luna was in there. What if it's some property of your shared DNA?"

"Ok, but what if it's universal, everywhere. And maybe our shared DNA makes it easier to see."

"Right, that could be true, too. So we can test that. You and Savi go in, Tanya tries to join you. See if you can connect with the bodies."

"Right. They can be ready for when we get there? You remember what happened?"

Save looked at me. "Yes, I remember it perfectly. Everything was cloudy and hard to think about. You took your own blood and you annointed my eyes. And suddenly everything was visible. I could see it. "

I sat down and held his hands. It was real.

"And one more thing." Rik looked over at me. "Maybe you can find Cerrone."

"Do you think she's like me?" I hadn't thought much about her since we met her. "Why?"

"Think about it. If she can access the red place, she can help. She can help free them all."

I looked at Savi, "Do you think that's possible?"

He took a deep breath, "I don't know. I think so. What happened with me, I think it could happen to any of us. I can feel Tee and Luna. I felt it when they woke up. I just couldn't get them. I couldn't get to them."

"So maybe I can find Cerrone in there?

"I think it's worth a try." Rik looked over at Savi. Savi seemed to agree.

***

I sat in the pit and closed my eyes. I put my left hand into Tanya's and my right into Savi's. They held hands, too. This group of three of us was going to try to pierce through to the red space.

I pressed my eyes together tightly, waiting for the red light to show through from the black. I breathed in. I saw white shapes in the black as I squeezed, resolving into jagged shapes. They began to fade and then shifted to red and remained consistent. They seemed to throb in the space around and began to breathe with that faith flicker that I remembered, the one that suggested a far away fire. I looked to my right and saw Savi. His body was brown and thick and meaty, bearlike, full of the machines of creation and growth, birth, the hunt.

He was strong and that strength seemed to radiate out of him, forward, like a ray of reddish light emanating from his chest. He turned to me. His eyes were dark and sharp now, aware, focused. He was erect and his cock was jutting up from his legs, pointing upward, leaning against his sweaty belly, his midsection. He was life, in so many ways, powerful, growing, building.

I looked down at myself as the red built around me, like tiles shifting in, filling the space more and more. My skin was lighter than his, olive, smooth, dripping sweat in the rawness of the red. In the red, we were all bodies first and I was no exception.

There were no thoughts in this place, nothing civilized. There were dinosaur brain emotions and belly hunches, Thick sensory dumps from the core of your body.

My tits were dancing in the faraway fires, Nipples erect and wanting. I imagined them free to let go and to drip milk down my belly, covering me, blessing me with the sweet rites of release. My belly was full and, If I listened closely, I could feel inside a possibility. I closed my eyes even tighter and saw a tiny light within me. This time, there would be no bleeding. My body held tight to the tiny spark as I sat cross legged, grabbing onto it with all the strength it could muster. I blew on the spark, fanning it. It felt like familiar energy. It was me and it was Meijo, both of us. Infinitesimally small, waiting.

I looked to my left and saw Tanya. She was red, pink, perfect. Her hair was almost shockingly red, flowing down over her head, pouring over her back, nearly reaching the tips of her breasts, with nipples so crimson red that they almost lit the space around us. I could see the brilliant line with tiny hairs running down her belly, dipping into the space of her belly button, connecting to the tuft of bright red hair topping the bright raw red lips of her cunt.

There was so much energy in her, so much to be released.

Her eyes were closed.

This wasn't her place. As remarkable as her body was, she was someone built for higher spaces. She was brain and soul and intellect, pureness, wisdom, ascendent. Her place wasn't in the red. She had a lovable body but she wasn't of the body. She was a thing of the mind.

I smelled them both next to me, filling my senses. They were magnificent. I used their energy to reach out farther. I had never gone anywhere else in the red. I stood up and felt my form beneath me. It felt savage and powerful. I felt alive, my skin was lit under a thousand fires and it felt electric. The sweat poured from me and my nipples leaked. I was wet and horny and transcendent and prowling across the center of life. I saw thick red threads above me, reaching out.

A thread connect to Savi, attaching itself to his body like an umbilical cord. It undulated and moved, crawling between his legs, pushing inside him. A cord, thick and alive, dropped from the entangled mass above me and reached out to Tanya. She slowly spread her legs and put her hands under her ass. Her thick, ruddy pussy lips spread open and the cord slipped inside, filling her, connecting her.

A cord dropped from above. This was the snake from the Bible. I saw it now. This wasn't some satanic animal and there was no apple. The cord descended, wet, pulsing. I wrapped my fist around it and let it explore me. I was aware in the red, but I needed to be all-seeing in this space.

I needed connection. Ths was the knowledge delivered by the snake.

The cord made its way down my body, wrapping around my engorged tits, snaking down the slick round belly, and it connected to my clit. I stopped and spread my legs while the cord delivered an electrical current to my clit, building, burrowing, slinking into my open cunt and spreading it open.

It slid inside, deeper and deeper until it had passed the point where I could feel it. I pulled the cord close and licked it, feeling the sweat that had built on it. My belly felt full as it wrapped itself and curled within me. I was a receptor, a receiver of life. And when I opened my eyes, in the red, red light poured out, illuminating a world of thick crimson skeins like veins wrapping around the world. I could see bodies everywhere.

I could see Tee and Luna. They were awake. They felt me connecting. I could feel their panic, but their passion. I could feel their want. As the lights flickered across the endless bodies I saw the powerful bodies in stasis, thousands of them. Not just at LifeQuest here, but all across the country.

It was overwhelming.

I was grateful for my weight, for my size, my mass, in the red where my body spoke for me, elevating me. I felt the cord between my leg and rubbed it, connecting to my dinosaur brain, the oldest vertebrate stem, a place I could kiss and tell my body I loved her. I could hold her and make her feel like she was enough, like she was worth loving.

I started laughing as the cord pulsed in and out of me, realising I was so full, in so many ways.

And then I saw her.

Kneeling in the red, surrounded by the flickering lights, her skin was obsidian, a precious gem but sweaty, liquid, perfect. Her hair fell down her back in neat cornrows. I could taste her from here, the sweaty mess between her legs as she knelt in the red, as I had. It pulled me toward her. I never realized how brilliant her eyes were.

I kneeled next to her, taking in her smell like an animal. I breathed in her body and wanted her.

She filled up my vision.

And then she turned to look right at me, and I heard the melody of her voice ring out across the red.

"And who the fuck are you?"

Gone

First of all, to be absolutely honest, no, Bron was not more tolerable more feminine. He was a squealing, crying, raging baby, freaking out and throwing up all over until Savi grabbed the syringe and shot him up again. He dragged him back to the back bedroom.

Rik sighed. "Is this our long term management solution for him from now on?"

Tanya perked up. The place was trashed from Bron's 4-minute long rage across the entire house. "Just until we do this, then we can drop him back off.

Meijo was thinking it through, "Then he tells everyone what happened? and shows them? Or does he? What do we think?"

"Is it more embarrassing for him or worse for us?" Emmi was following. It was just hard to imagine how people like him thought.

"I Honestly don't know." I thought. "I mean, he extorted me for sex. I think that's illegal." I tried to do anything to face the real issue. but there it was. "I guess we know without a doubt now. I'm causing it. I'm turning people into biological women?"

"How far does that go?" Rik looked curious. "M, do you feel like a woman?"

Miejoclosed his eyes and scrunched up his face. "I don't feel *wrong* like this. But I don't know. Man, woman, it's cultural right?"

Tanya nodded, "absolutely. The brian is physical and it has something to say about it. Does your brain feel like a woman now?"

"My brain feels the same. But not. The back part of my brain feels like this is normal. Does that make sense?"

Savi walked back in, "he's comfortable. I think. I really don't know how anyone else feels. I've been alive for a day or two."

I pointed, "Exactly. Exactly. This is what I think." I wanted to Remind Savi for a minute that NONE of us knows how anyone else feels.

He was not the weirdo. And neither was Meijo.

In reality, I was

"I have to tell you guys, thought," Tanya slid into the pit and looked up, "That was maybe the most fucked up, cool, bizarre thing ever. Amazing. It was like being in the center of everything. like this is life, fuckers."

"I appreciate you doing it with me." I smiled at her.

"But you're right. I can't do anything in that space. I'm a visitor, I think. For now. But I want to learn. I feel like if I got more in touch with the animal part of me, I could do it." Tanya wasn't good at not being good at something.

"But Cerrone?" Rik slid in next to her.

"She is going to meet us at the hotel across from LifeQuest where Eiko is meeting us. We're going to try together from there, along with Savi. She calls that place 'the inside'."

Tanya shook her head "I prefer 'the red'. It feels like that to me, red, raw, primal. Like we're prowling like an animal." In it, she seemed somehow less civilized. her hair even looked wilder.

Savi moved over behind Rik and grabbed his head. He seemed wilder, too. it was something i could feel in me. the longer you were in there the more red and raw you felt. Rik reached up and put his arms around him pulling him over the back of the couch. They laughed as Rik leaned in to kiss him.

I guess we had time for all of that.

Tanya looked over at Rik."You know, none of us have ever seen you bottom before."

Rik waved his hand, "That's not true."

I remembered. "It actually is true. You sucked off Tee while I was in her body, but I never saw you actually bottom."

"Well, we don't have to be at the hotel until later, so good luck, fuckers," he grabbed Savi's hand and the two started off toward the front bedroom.

"Boooo" Tanya threw a pillow at him.

"If you do it here, on the KOZO, so they can watch, I'll get everyone off and won't even watch." The part of my brain that was the temple whore was still active, it seemed, I wanted to be of use badly.

"So, you'll be the mouthbitch for everyone if I take it up the ass?" Rik was playing. You could tell he was up for it.

'No one even has to talk to me. I'll behave."

"And they can do whatever they want to get off on your face and you'll just suck it up like a whore?"

"Anything, I promise." This was Rik acting out to get me hot. These were the words. He is so evil. I keep forgetting that he's been my friend for longer than anyone. And for all that time, we've been the devil on each other's shoulders.

Such a valuable job.

Tanya pulled me down in front of her. Her newfound rawness from our journey in the red seemed to be making her horny. She pulled her shirt off and pushed her panties down. They were black and thin and I felt all my senses kick in. She pushed my face into her panties, forcing my nose down. She smelled alive and powerful.

It was a pretty smell, a musky beautiful one. I tried to close my eyes, though and let it take over. I could see the wetness glistening in her panties as she held them to my face and I sucked them. It was electric on my lips, sleek and cool and wet. I tried to clean them spotlessly, licking and sucking at the fabric while the warm wetness of her pussy itself dripped down on my forehead, rubbing against me.

She pulled my face up and pressed it against her cunt, rubbing herself on my and compressing my nose inside her. I felt the thickness of her lips under my tongue and lost all semblance of thought.

Wetness pooled inside her and I used my tongue like a spoon, pulling it all out of her into my waiting mouth. Rik and Savi's moans pulled at my attention, but I focused on Tanya. She pulled my face out and let her panties fall to the ground. She put her fingers inside herself, releasing a small pool of liquid into her palm. I dug in like an animal, sucking at it, drinking it all up.

I sucked her hand and pussy dry and felt more liquid fill the deep well between her lips as my reward. Under the thin tuft of red hair I found the front tip of her cunt and played my tongue across it, feeling the little, red button of her clit. I wanted it so bad. I tried to restrain myself, but Tanya released me, pushing herself into my face hard, holding my head there. She jacked off against my face, rubbing her clit on me like I was some kind of a vibrator.

She lifted her ass up and turned my head around so I was leaning backward, making sure everything leaking out of her landed on me, covering my face, my mouth. She leaned forward and I could feel her weight on my face as she waterboarded me. There was so much, I choked, begging wordlessly that she wouldn't stop. I didn't know if she was cumming or pissing or both but I didn't care.

All I wanted was for her to satisfy herself in my mouth, to use my face for her fuck. She pushed down and let go and there was a rush of thick liquid filling me. I opened my mouth as wide as possible and sucked at her. She leaned over and grabbed my tits, still falling out of my robe, as hard as she could.

She punished my nipples, squeezing so hard, twisting and ripping at them while she came over and over in my mouth. Her breath mixed with the grunts of Rik and Savi fucking and it all sounded like a beautiful wordless song.

Sitting up a little she laid her asshole on my mouth. I could feel her reach behind her and spread her ass while she rubbed it in my face. I licked at it, digging my tongue in her while she slowed down and then, eventually, slid off me.

I looked up, the room spinning around me, to see Savi's thick prick invading Rik's ass on the KOZO. He was pumping slowly, pressing the impossibly long shaft into him while Rik arched his back and groaned, letting it pierce him so deeply that I imagined I could see the shape of it writhing around in his belly. I felt Emmi's hands behind me, holding my head, grabbing me. My head lolled backward and she kissed me, stealing away some of the precious liquid on my lips from Tanya's brilliant red raw pussy.

Emmi's fist wrapped in my hair and I felt a rush of pain as she yanked my head back toward her, pressing my face into her root. She had lifted her legs up and was squatting on the couch, her cunt wide open, atop the precious little hole of her ass. I extended my tongue to dig it into her ass and play with my pretty girl's pink opening.

She pressed my face into it.

I started making out with her ass and I could feel her opening and closing it, making out with me in return. Something overwhelmed me just at that moment, the idea that we could kiss like this, and i was so passionately in love, so in heat, just wanting to kiss my partner, To stick my tongue inside them and make out, to be one connected by our extending wanting holes, licking, eating, me fucking that hole with my wet red tongue.

She slammed her ass down in my face, passionately, more loving than Tanya did but still with urgency, with immediacy. The thing I loved about Emmi was that she wielded her pussy like a man. When she had to cum, she didn't hold back. She pushed it, pressed it, shoved it down your throat.

She was an animal that needed release when her slit was vibrating and that is all I needed, just to know, just to be told what to do. She rubbed my face in her as I latched onto her clit, sucking it across the full length of it, pulling it in my mouth.

The room was filled with the sounds of Savi and Rik fucking each other's asses, and I recorded every slap of thigh against a waiting ass, every sucking in of the other's cock. Emmi came in my open mouth and pushed me on the ground. She shoved her bare foot in my mouth. I took it in and tried to get it as far down my throat as I could.

From the corner of my eye, I watched Savi grab Rik's arms and pull them back like a Greek wrestler while he jammed his meat as far as he could up the his hole from behind. Rik grunted and squirmed, his own dick dripping pre-cum, hard and sticky against the back of the KOZO as Savi let out a yell and unleashed a torrent of hot cum up his open ass. I put my hand between my legs and rubbed as hard as I could, feeling Emmi's pretty toenails scratching the back of my throat.

If only I could get the whole thing down my throat.

She pushed me down and kicked me, connecting with my left tit. I got on my hands and knees like a cow, like an animal to be handled roughly and she got up and kicked me again. Over and over she brought her bare foot up against my tit and connected, causing bright white sparks of pain to glow across my closed eyes. I thanked her, softly, crying from the release, more than from the pain.

Rik was breathing hard, lying there, laughing with Savi, who still had his dick stuffed far up inside him. His arms fell off the KOZO in a way that showed how tired he was.

Exhausted.

I rolled over on the ground and Meijo kissed me lightly. I opened my mouth and gratefully felt his tongue in it. It was so different, yet so familiar. His face, usually covered in a light stubble, was smooth and sleek and I didn't care either way. It was him.

He pulled off the shirt and pants and stood over me. I hadn't realized how beautiful his new body was. To me it looked flawless. He will, even now, point out places where it's not enough, where it doesn't meet the expectations people might have.

But I never saw any of that. I didn't before and I don't now. I reached up and grabbed his ass and pulled it down. I centered his ass on my face so that my mouth made perfect contact with his clit and my nose and face slid up into his waiting asshole. He fit my face so perfectly, but he always did. He leaned forward and held onto my tits.

I remembered everything I felt while in the red and spread my legs for him, letting him see the wet mess I was from servicing them all. He moved down my body and placed his face between my legs.

Suddenly, I realized that the blocks against me doing this had all fallen away. I didn't want to push anyone away again. And Meijo was just tall enough to slide his mouth perfectly onto me, clamping onto my own clit and sucking at me.

I instantly felt it all across me. In my chest, in my stomach, in my arms I could feel it. My cunt felt huge, wide open, waiting for him as he rode my face and shoved his mouth between my legs. Time began to fall away and I inhaled the smell of him so deeply. Despite everything, he really still smelled like Meijo. It was really him.

And that time, when I came, I cried so hard that I felt like it would go on forever. I felt open and realized how prone to crying I was over the last few days.

And I cried some more.

***

Rik was still naked but he was now clicking through the channels on the active wall in front of us, trying to find something calming.

Admittedly, there was so little calming.

The news showed a series of protests across the country. Men's groups had gotten together to protest the Senza Dolore. I wasn't sure what policies they were protesting and, honestly, looking at the signage, I think they weren't either.

The idea of women in charge was the core of the protests. Most of them were peaceful, but there had been open marches and protests in twelve of the seventeen states. I had always thought of Baja as so advanced, compared to other places, that it was hard for me to watch what was happening.

Here. Rik stopped on a channel and Tanya took a deep breath, pulling a pillow in front of her.

"Damn."

Rik nodded. "Damn is right. You know where that is, right?" I looked around. Meijo had gone back to take a shower. Emmi and Savi seemed half asleep on the couch. I wasn't sure how worried to be.

"That is just our luck." I sighed. This protest didn't look too much different than many of the others. And it was being held in a place that made sense, I guess. It was exactly half a block away from the center for gender studies that the Senza Dolore used as a headquarters, which was about ten doors down from The Milia Grazia hotel, the place where were meant to meet Eiko and Cerrone tomorrow morning.

Which was directly across the street from LifeQuest.

People were relatively calm. It was mostly men waving signs, speaking out angrily. This protest had been going on since early this afternoon, we saw, and it showed no sign of slowing down.

"If this is still going on tomorrow, we are going to have to walk right through it." Tanya said.

"I don't understand why they can't just do this a few doors down."

I was starting to get worried. I remembered a few hours ago when this thing tomorrow seemed so easy.

"It was probably easier to get a permit in front of a hotel. Like, that entire area is probably zoned for it." Rik tossed the remote onto the couch.

"Ok, how bad do we think this is?" I watched the screen. Some of the men involved seemed rational, reasonable. Like regular people. One or two speakers looked enraged. The sound was down so I couldn't hear them but they looked ready to explode.

"It's a five, I think." Rik crossed his arms. His cock dangled comfortably between his legs and i thought, not for the first time, by the way, that there should be a whole different name for a dick that wasn't hard. Like a soft one should be called "Enrique" and a hard one is just "The COCK" in all caps.

"It's a seven. I think that there will be a lot of police out by tomorrow. And we will look suspicious." Tanya shook her head.

I looked around. I guess we looked suspicious. We all really just looked sleepy. I was in pain, but it was that good kind of pain that you experienced when you went through something cool. Like when you run a marathon and get a huge pain in your chest afterward and you feel like you might die, but you know you won't, you just need to go to bed.

"I think it's less. I think we're going to be ok. In all honesty, this could be something we could blend in with afterward." I had no idea how many bodies we would be talking about. Suddenly I wondered if they would have clothes on. This might be harder than I thought.

"Holy…" Rik turned up the volume. Suddenly I heard a familiar voice. I looked down at Emmi and put my hand on her head. "Can you grab Meijo?"

She nodded and bounced off to the back bedroom.

Tanya's eyes were wide. "Is that who I think it is?"

On the dias, speaking loudly, was Mika Spencer. With shorter hair.

But very much alive.

We listened.

"Many of them have that ability. And different ones. I never asked for this. Inside I am a man. But I'll never be one again. And the woman responsible is free to walk around today and do it over and over again. That woman is Seka Ogurd."

He waved a photograph of me, clearly visible, as the ground chanted and screamed,

But I didn't care. I fell onto my knees. There had been a bus on my shoulders since that night. It was huge, but it was gone now.

For the 20th time that night, I started to cry.

He was alive. I didn't kill him. Somehow, he was alive.

I mentally adjusted my murder rate to zero, reaching out to the active wall. I looked back and saw Tanya's face. She was confused. Emmi ran back into the room.

"They're gone. Meijo. That guy, Bron. They're both gone.

Gone.

Fruitflies

According to the Kunal Notebooks, In the early 2000s, there was a researcher named David Featherstone who worked with Fruit Flies to try to determine certain genetic body and behavior models. His team made some interesting breakthroughs.

Fruit Flies were popular for genetic research for a number of reasons. They only have four pairs of chromosomes and a relatively simple genome. Not too hard to pull apart. They also have a ten-day life cycle, which makes them easy to model, mold, evaluate, then move on to the next generation. And despite their simplicity, they are very similar to humans. In fact, about 60% of their genome is the same as humans. They are cheap, they reproduce quickly. They have a cool name: Drosophila Melanogaster. There were a lot of fun things to learn from them.

One of those things was the discovery of a gene they called GB or "Gender blind."

GB transports the neurotransmitter glutamate to brain cells. Altering levels of glutamate change the strength of nerve cell junctions, called synapses, which play a key role in human and animal behavior.

The interesting thing about GB is that it can be attached to various other genes and triggered. And when it is triggered, that fruit fly variant will become gay.

Well, not exactly gay. But they won't distinguish between males and females anymore. Let's say bisexual. The males will just court other males, have intercourse with them, treat them like females.

To test this, the researchers genetically altered synapse strength, independent of GB. They also gave flies drugs to alter synapse strength. As predicted, they were able to turn fly homosexuality on and off, within hours.They were even able to attach this behavior to things like time or climate. In one case, making it so that the Fruit flies became gay once the temperature rose above 75 degrees.

It might seem like I'm rambling, but I give you this information now so that you will understand better when we meet Maya Greene, another person from the LifeQuest files we found at Djinn Maretti's.

***

We had spent the entire night looking for Meijo. Bron must have grabbed him but we didn't know where he was, either. Everyone was trying to make me feel like it wasn't my fault but it was.

Finally, at six a.m., we went to the Milia Grazia hotel for an early check in. The place was beautiful and made up to look like an old Renaissance parlor. Ordinarily, Meijo and I would have enjoyed it, at least a little. But his absence wasn't the only thing marring this visit.

"So, you're saying that my account was declined?"

The young man at the counter looked like the kind of person who didn't enjoy new things happening. And he wasn't enjoying this. "It says you don't have the money. Is there a different account you want us to use?"

"Can you try it again?" Since I was twelve years old I had never experienced anything like this. At first it seemed like it must be a mistake.

"I've tried it three times."

Rik stepped up, "Let me do this."

I looked at him, "It's a lot of money."

"I'm sure. You know I haven't spent anything on anything for the last 10 years. I live in the back of my classroom. I stay at your place 99% of the time. Do you know how much money I have saved up?"

"What the hell is going on?"

"Ma'am, it just says that the account is empty."

I looked up at Rik. he tried to calm me down. "ok, another mystery to solve. That's all."

He paid. We checked in and went up to the room. It was on the seventh floor looking across to LifeQuest. The protest had died down considerably, but it looked like people were still assembling.

And they were building a bigger stage.

This wasn't going anywhere.

I looked around the room. It was large and fun looking. I imagined the depraved use we could have put this place to. Savi was carrying the bag we had brought with us, and Tanya and Rik were looking around the place for listening devices or anything. Meijo's disappearance had made me and Emmi sad but it had energized Those two to treat this like a real thing with real stakes.

We were all processing it in our way.

I kept sending messages to Miejo and so far, none had come back. I kept my personal phone on vibrate and readied myself for anything.

Emmi was calling around to all our friends, still holding out hope that Miejo had just been overwhelmed and had left on his own. I tried to make myself believe that.

And that's where we all were when the knock on the door came.

I looked at Rik. We didn't have a gun. We didn't have a weapon at all.

We had nothing.

And Cerrone wasn't going to be here until 10am.

Who was at the door?

I moved to the door and looked through the opening to see who it might be. All I could see was the hallway. I shrugged at Rik and pulled the door open.

"You know, it's a great carpet out there, but it's a weird line, you know, in the hallway. They make the carpets so that you don't notice the dirt, but the optical effects are fucked, honestly."

An older man of about 80 with a mop of white hair moved in like a whirlwind. He reached out to Rik who was closest.

"Heyo. I'm Djinn Maretti. Good to meet you."

I stepped up closer to him and he turned and smiled.

"Hey, Peanut. I can tell by the eyebrows, you're Seka." He leaned in out of habit, as though talking to a young person. "You're still as pretty as you ever were."

Emmi stepped up to defend me as he pulled me in for a hug. He looked at her.

"Just a little hug" He hugged me tightly. I'm not going to say I didn't need it. I put my head down on his neck and hugged him back. He smelled like ancient aftershave and it was nice.

"Oh, and where's my manners?" He reached out the door and ushered in a girl of about nineteen.

She looked shy, quiet. She was dark-skinned with short cropped curly hair. She had a nose piercing on the left side and was dressed in black. She was thick, curvy, and pretty. Her smile, when it happened, was so dazzling white in the middle of her face it radiated.

Emmi smiled widely at her, trying to coax one out of her, recognizing her black eyeliner.

They were two of a kind.

The girl smiled back. There we go.

"And this is Maya Greene."

Rik spoke up, "That was one of the other names. Maya Greene."

"From my records, yes. And oh." He felt his pockets looking for something. "Here we go." He handed me a thick envelope. "We had to cancel your trust this morning. I'm sure you can use it."

It was bloated and full of cash. Large bills. I couldn't tell you how much was in it.

"You canceled her trust fund?" Tanya came to my defense.

"Well, I had no choice. I could see you booked this room, originally. Anything I can see, they can see. I think you want to be under the radar here."

Emmi looked over at him. "Why did you bring this young lady?" She nodded at Maya.

"Oh. She is a recent find by LifeQuest. But I'm doing my best now to keep her under the radar, too. Kill two birds as they say." He winked.

"What do we do?" I looked confused, I'm sure.

"The records list her as an Idemomorph. I don't know about these things. But Cerrone will. Cerrone is coming, too, right?"

I nodded. "Why are you doing this?"

He stood up straight. "I've been working for LifeQuest for almost 50 years now. I've been piecing together what's going on, but I realized a while ago, I'm not not smart enough to see the big picture. I know numbers, and I know people.

Through it all, the only thing I can do is to try to keep the people safe and make the numbers work. You know? And I think she's safe with you." He waved at Maya.

She looked up at me defiantly, as if to say she was going to pay her own way. I smiled at her.

He knelt down and hugged her. "Maya. You listen to Seka and Cerrone. And if I can, I promise I'm gonna see you again." He stood up to leave.

I ran out the door, "Wait. You can't stay? And help or something?"

His eyes were kind but there was something sad behind them. I saw it now.

"I think LifeQuest might be thinking I'm reaching the end of my usefulness. I'd best be away from you. But before I go, you should know it wasn't your fault."

"What wasn't?"

He grabbed my hand. "That boy liked you. And you really liked him. And you were just kids. You were just playing doctor, you know, in the back yard. You didn't do anything wrong. You're a good person. I watched you."

He let go of my hand and made his way down the hallway. "I watched you." he made a motion pointing to his eyes before he turned into the stairwell and disappeared. At that moment, my phone vibrated. I looked down.

And we started planning.

***

I explained everything I knew now to the group. Emmi was doing her best to make sure Maya felt like she fit in, but I still didn't see why, in the big picture, she was here. But she was someone to protect right now and this room seemed safe as anywhere could be.

Savi and I went down to the lobby to grab breakfast food to bring up for everyone while Rik and Tanya planned.

The more I talked to Savi, the more familiar his demeanor seemed. I saw parts of me in him, but also parts of Emmi. It was strange hearing him talk, with that deep, masculine baritone with Emmi's enthusiasm.

"Eating as me is so strange. Like, I think I like omelets. This body. But I never would have known.

"Well, I love them, so I think that is very rational and wise. Are you a cheese or no-cheese?"

He closed his eyes, "I feel like I'm a cheese."

"Again, you seem to have this all figured out. Very smart."

"I wanted to tell you something."

I started piling cinnamon rolls onto a plate. This will be well received. "Shoot."

"I'm immune to you."

I looked at him and it took me a second to process. "Immune?"

"When we were all together. I mean, I didn't have sex with you but your... juices were all over me. And I didn't change."

"Oh, my god, I'm so sorry." I didn't realize that he had come into contact with me like that. But Meijo did have me all over him and He was hanging on to both me and Savi tightly.

"No, don't be. That's what I'm telling you. It doesn't affect me. Something about our connection. Our shared biology. But I can feel it, you know?"

"You can feel it?"

"Yes, there is power in you. It's so much. And it's not just that. That Maya girl has power, too."

"You can feel that, too?"

"Not like with you. You and I are connected. We are part of something in the red."

I looked at him. There is something I was feeling he understood. "I just wanted to know where I came from, what secret thing I came from. But you, and Luna, and Tee, you are also branches of my tree, I guess."

"I know." He was balancing so much food on his plates.

"It sounds dumb, but I can't breathe right until they are ok."

We made our way back up to the room. "And that's how I know it."

"How you know what?"

"That we're going to be all right. That this is going to work."

He leaned down and kissed me. It was a gentle kiss, but a real one. I opened my mouth and leaned into it. In other circumstances this might have been a "let's start fooling around" kiss. Here, it was very obviously a "I'm in 100% for what is needed" kiss.

And it was amazing.

I opened the door and gave Eiko a hug. It looked like everyone had shown up while we were gone.

Cerrone was there with the woman who had "guarded her" at the club - the woman with the Senza Dolore tattoo. I smiled at them both.

"I think we've exceeded occupancy with this room." I joked.

"I already did that one." Emmi gave me a kiss and started taking plates of food, moving them to the long side table.

"So, my work is done here." I looked over at Cerrone. She cautiously stepped over toward me.

"We talked in the inside. I never had a full conversation there."

I smiled, "Yeah, it's not really the place to intellectualize."

She laughed and shook her head. She seemed more open here than at the club, more herself. She put her hand on my stomach and I covered it with mine.

I wondered who else saw that.

The woman with her leaned in. She was light skinned, possibly Indian. Her hair was short and dyed blonde. It would have been hard to place her. "It's her. She's the Karyomorph."

I held my hand out. "I'm Seka. Can you tell? Can you see it?"

The woman held out her hand. "I'm Rana. Rana Khemani. And no. I can't tell. But I think she can. I'm just a baseline human."

"Is Seka not a human?" Tanya interjected.

Cerrone looked over at her, "I don't know. I'm just finding out about this, honestly. I always sort of knew about myself deep down. But they know more." She pointed to Rana

"Rana is Senza Dolore" I explained.

"From the club. Right." Rik reached over to start eating. Everyone was on edge, I could tell.

Emmi was fascinated. "So you know what Seka can do?"

"I can't control it."

"Yes. You are one of a number of mutations."

"Me, too?" Maya blurted out. i could tell she needed answers.

Rana took her hand. "Yes."

"But she's still human. A human being?" Eiko was trying to wrap his head around it all.

Cerrone stood up straight," of course. We all are. We're human beings. Just not regular ones."

"So, Your group has been following us, the mutations?" I asked Rana.

"As much as we can. These are complicated times. Once everyone out there finds out just exactly what is going on, it's going to get, well... even more complicated. Men will strike out. They will assume it's intentional."

"So you didn't want people to find out, either?" Rik asked.

"I assume you're referring to them," She pointed in the direction of LifeQuest.

Tanya identified them, "LifeQuest."

"I don't know what they know. But we should find out today."

Emmi was at the window, "What is happening today? It looks like yesterday but bigger. More people are gathering."

Rana looked toward the window. "Today the head of LifeQuest, Vero Kaine, is supposed to make an historic speech. About the future."

Eiko looked out the window, "Shit."

"Senza Dolore will be here, a lot of us." Rana continued.

"What is he going to say?" I asked.

She sighed, "We don't know. But we suspect that if he says what we think he will, it's going to be ugly. A match on a powderkeg"

Rik nodded, "And we need to get those bodies out of there before that happens."

"All of them," Cerrone clarified. I breathed out. I realized that I had been holding my breath, afraid that no one would see how important this was. I nodded at Cerrone and she stared back.

"Every one." I affirmed.

Eiko asked, "How ugly are we talking? A riot?"

Rana breathed out heavily, "Maybe. Some of it depends on his tone, this Vero Kaine."

"But some people here, they have powers?" Emmi sounded like she was trying to manufacture hope.

Rana nodded, "yes. In a way."

Tanya asked, "Well, we know what Seka can do." she nodded to Cerrone. "What does she do?"

Cerrone looked around the room. She moved toward the bedroom and called out. A child stepped out, holding her hand, wearing a black hoodie pulled down. Cerrone stepped into the middle of the room. She knelt down and pulled the hoodie down.

Underneath was a 5 year old girl with curly black hair and deep Black skin. She was very pretty. But a familiar pretty. As Cerrone stood back up it became clear that the two shared exactly the same face, with every detail replicated perfectly. Just slighty smaller.

Rik turned to us. "Parthenogenisis. That's what a Geniploid is."

Eiko looked confused, "What's that?"

I knelt down and smiled at the little girl, offering her my hand. "I'm Seka."

She smiled and shook my hand. "I'm Mianne."

Rik looked over at his brother. "Mianne is from a virgin birth. Cerrone didn't need a partner to get pregnant. That's her mutation."

Tanya stepped over to Rana, "So what are we about to hear from the head of LifeQuest? What is he going to say?"

Rana sighed, "If I had to guess. He's going to tell them about these mutations. What we think they add up to. All different, mostly. But more every day. Each one pointing in the same direction."

"And what is that," Eiko asked.

"That the world, the earth, is phasing out men. That it's making them obsolete. And with each new mutation it is getting closer and closer to a biological system that doesn't need them"

"That doesn't need men?" Emmi looked over.

Rana finished, "Where men are not necessary for the survival of the species."

Eiko paused. "Fuck."

Tanya raised her hand, "But, wait. gender is a construct, sure, but even biological gender is a spectrum - a continuum. What is nature doing?"

Rik spoke up, "If I had to guess, it's more of a pruning. If you think of bilogical sex with very male over here and very female over here on the spectrum, it's just clipping it here." He made a motion with his hand, "Or here." it's biology so it's sloppy.

I looked out the window, scanning the stage. "There. There they are." I pointed.

People were beginning to assemble on the stage, in seats, as though they would be speaking or offering support. At the far end of the stage were two familiar people.

Meijo and Bron looked uncomfortable as they slid into their seats.

Cerrone looked out. "Who are they?"

I stood up, pointing to Meijo. "That's my boyfriend."

Cerrone squinted. She looked at us.

"I am so fucking confused."

Two Hours

"No." Rana folded her arms.

"What do you mean, no?" Cerrone seemed a bit confused but really more angry.

"I mean, no, I don't leave you alone. That's not my job."

"Your job? Up until yesterday, I thought your job was to be my girlfriend."

"And it is, baby. I am. But I also have a job to do."

"Bullshit." Cerrone pulled away.

"Ok, baby, I am with you. I am. But I'm also Senza Dolore. And I need to make sure nothing happens to you and Mia."

"Is that your job? Is that why you hooked up with me in the first place?"

"My feelings for you are real."

Cerrone put her hand up and looked at me. "She can't go wth the other group because I'm her job, apparently."

"Wait, I need you to go with the rescue team so we can stay as the "sensory" team." I didn't really know how to explain that any better.

Savi looked over, "I can go with the rescue team."

"I really wanted you with me in the red."

"You have Cerrone and now Maya." Rik pointed out. Is that enough?"

I thought. "I guess it's going to have to be."

Eiko called out, "Hey, guys. I think we may have just gotten lucky."

I liked the sound of that. On the stage now, in the middle of the men assembling, were 40 or 50 men, dressed as guards, swarming around Vero Kaine, protecting him.

"So, if they have a shitload of guards protecting that guy..." Eiko mused.

"Who is protecting LifeQuest itself?" Rik continued.

"Right." His brother concurred.

***

I admit, I love the fact that we may have caught a break. But that really only meant that what he was about to say was bad.

Really bad. Like "I need protection" bad. The current unrest between men and women required less than a full blown spark. It required just a little bad.

I looked at Eiko, "How do you feel about this? This idea that earth may be phasing out men?"

"I don't know. I don't know how to feel. I mean, I see Earth's point, but..."

"You don't love the idea of being obsolete."

"Right." He thought for a second. Eiko and I weren't as close as I was with his brother, but we'd had our moments.

He finished, "Look, I wasn't planning on having kids. That wasn't how I was contributing anyway. So maybe for me it's not so bad. Phasing me out genetically isn't going to stop me from writing a book about all this shit later. Or maybe it's a terrible movie."

Ok. that was not unhealthy. Good.

"We had to know this would happen." Rik continued. "I mean, when I was a kid, I used to have mice. I raised them. And no, lie, in order to keep them all healthy, you had to remove the males because they would always get violent. Maybe it's time for the universe to do that. Maybe God is just thinning out the males in the cage."

"Well, I think it's shit," Emmi interjected. "There are lots of men I think are great, and I don't care for the planet making my long-term dating decisions for me."

I considered that.

It was fair.

4:00 PM

Bron turned to Meijo, seated amidst a group of men. "Just stay close." The stage was leaning to one side, awkward, with a mess of folding chairs and random LifeQuest banners. You could tell that this wasn't an event anyone had planned until fairly recently.

"That's him?" Meijo pointed to Kaine, getting ready to speak.

"Yep, that's the money right there. You stick close."

Meijo whispered, "What did you tell him?"

Bron looked around and leaned in. His breath was always hot for some reason. Some people are like that

"Your story is the same as mine, same as that Spencer chick's. I have fucking boobs now. They're not terrible and they're actually kind of fucking growing on me, but That's what these people need to be afraid of, right?"

"So, in his mind, we're examples?" Meijo looked at Kaine. He was a slight man, not large. His hair was white and thinning at top.

"Damn right. New ideas, new products, it works when you have a reason. He has a reason now. He's got it all figured out, he thinks. Just stay close."

Mika was sitting near the podium. She would be one of the first to speak again. Meijo pointed at her, "She seems totally fine. I don't understand. We saw her die."

Bron smiled awkwardly. The men around them had given them a wide berth. "It looks like the strategy has changed. There is no more keeping it a secret. People like her were a liability. Now they're an asset. They probably planned for it to happen one day. LifeQuest is pretty good at keeping fuckers alive if they need to."

Meijo sat uncomfortably next to him. I looked out the window.

He was so small, I could barely see him.

4:15 PM

Rana grabbed Mia. After some back and forth, she and Cerrone had decided she would stay in the hotel room with her and keep her safe. A priority we all agreed on.

Rick and Emmi were going to enter through the front. They were already on record there and had been there a number of times. Eiko, Tanya, and Savi were going to go around back and meet them inside. Hopefully the access that Bron had given them, coupled with Savi's understanding of the building, would give them a chance to locate and free the bodies.

All we needed to do was to wake them up, just as I had inadvertently with Savi. This time I would have help. Cerrone and Maya would be there with me.

Up on the roof.

We had decided that this would be the best approach. Being on the roof would let us potentially see what was happening while keeping us safe. We could block off the doorway to the upper corridor leading there, and then enter the red. And if everything went the way it was supposed to, we'd be done and back to the hotel room asap, no one the wiser.

And things always go like they're supposed to.

4:30 PM

"We should be together for this." Emmi put her arms around me in the bathroom.

I felt everything kind of all over the place and I knew what she meant. There were so many moving pieces for this. Being scattered all over felt really wrong for this. But I didn't see any other way.

"We will be. We're going to get Meijo back and free Luna and Tee and everyone and we're going to finish this."

She leaned in and kissed me on the mouth, her lips opening for me. I realized that we hadn't had the chance to figure out what we were, her and me and Meijo, and I hoped so hard that we would have that chance soon. I needed Meijo to be there when I told her I loved her.

I put my hands on her waist and kissed her back. I pushed harder and she leaned back, letting go.

There was so much letting go to do.

We had a few minutes and I sank into her.

Emmi and I had developed a kind of physical shorthand. When one of us pushed, the other one gave. And if the other one pushed, they were in charge.

It was simple and easy and it worked when Meijo was there, too. And it was interesting. It was a sexual dynamic that changed constantly but was always comfortable.

I put my hand between her legs, sliding it under her skirt and black panties. Her warmth was calming. It was an invitation. She was wet and soft and open and I pushed my fingers inside her as far as they would go. She spread her legs wider and pushed against me, making it all feel so intentional, so much the two of us, not just me.

She opened her mouth and I overtook it. Her arms dropped, falling backward. This was a giving pose. This was a position that was meant to make me feel like I could have anything.

I took her in and moved my hand back and forth, trying to press up against her little button inside until I heard that soft liquid sound that I loved so much. My hand filled up, slippery and electric. We were batteries, exchanging a charge perfectly, the wet between us creating a carrier for the current, keeping the sparks alive, vibrant, bouncing across our skin.

Even here with her I was desperate for a promise from the universe that everything would work out okay.

"I want to sleep with you inside me tonight, when this is all done," she whispered.

All I had to do was get through the next two hours.

4:35 PM

Cerrone, Maya, and I made our way up to the roof. We could still hear the speakers from down on the street, but they were muted a bit.

We put our hands together in a circle and sat down. Cerrone's hand was thin and elegant with strong calluses from working to make the club into something. I could feel her playing music, lifting weights, boxing. She was alive and she had put her hands through hell getting there.

Still, they felt supple and capable and responsive in my own.

Maya's hands were small and thick and so soft. They felt like the hands of someone more comfortable in the water. Someone who loved to dance and wave them about, expressive, warm, the hands of a lover. She could feel passion in her hands that was so intense it would move entire moons.

Both women felt so full of love and the freedom to express it.

I wondered what they felt from mine. But not in an awkward or self-conscious way. Just in a way that suggested me wanting to give them some part of me. I wondered if my hands felt like the love I had for my friends. If they felt like the version of me that I wanted to be, the compassionate person who was fixated on getting inside people's heads to find the thing to say or do that would make them bigger. I wondered if they felt like artists' hands or visionaries' hands or the kinds of hands that could tell a good story.

I wondered.

I looked up into the dense sunlight and closed my eyes. The sun dug through my pressed eyelids, projecting the red of my skin across my eyes in hiding. It was hard to see, at first, the distinction between black and red. I acclimated to it, though. And it became like a row of reddish beacons over my head, building a crimson organ for us to settle into.

I understood how Cerrone could call this the inside. I felt within something nurturing, something womblike. It was endless but not outdoors. It was just a type of body that could expand to devour and assimilate the world. In the red, I looked at Cerrone. Her skin was wet and silky looking, sleek, like a water animal, capable of incredible speeds because she was so dynamic and powerful. She moved her head and I could see the ribbons of muscle in her neck, so strong and powerful.

We faced LifeQuest and looked inside.

4:45 PM

The audience grew louder and louder. On stage right you could see guards milling around in their bright blue LifeQuest uniforms. A small contingent of police assembled across the stage as Vero Kaine stepped up into public view.

A smattering of people cheered. He was not a well-known man outside of media circles. He'd never been one of those pop media superstar CEOS or famous one-named billionaires. In his mind, he'd been a more serious man than that.

He waved to the people who did know who he was. Then, something chilling came from the loudspeaker, a portent of something still to come. Meijo looked down, realizing that the audience was almost exclusively men. Outside of the few on stage, there were no women anywhere.

None.

A booming voice rang out, "Gentlemen, please welcome the CEO and founder of LifeQuest, Vero Kaine!"

5:02 PM

Rik and Emmi sailed past the receptionist and stood outside the elevators on the third floor, with Rik 10,000 dollars poorer. They looked down to see the blue line, similar to the red one we had followed when we had first come there. They opened the door to the stairwell and propped it wide with a brick, just as they had with the bottom floor doors.

The halls were virtually empty, with the occasional person in a white coat moving back and forth. No one seemed to notice them as they entered the staging area. Neither one of them had ever seen anywhere but the launch rooms and Transition rooms. They thought they were prepared for what they might see.

But they weren't.

In a vast white room, thousands of bodies lined up, some nude, some covered in black underclothing. And, in front of them, in white coats, stood Eiko and Tanya.

And next to them, putting on white coats, were Luna and Tee.

Emmi grabbed white coats and they put them on.

"Are you guys ok?" Emmi looked up at Luna. She was so tall.

"I think so. I know you." She hugged Emmi.

"Where is Savi?" Rik asked

Tee was trying to look composed, "He's down at the end. He's trying to create a connection, like we had when we were...freed. It feels so strange. Like I woke up from a bunch of dreams."

Tanya buttoned her coat "No alarms, nothing. It looks like it's all business as usual."

"Well." Emmi smiled, "We're regular clients."

5:07 PM

Savi sat cross-legged inside LifeQuest, surrounded by rows of bodies. It was so easy to look in his direction, to let the red shift toward him. He looked up and there were red lights all around him, dancing around his caramel skin.

I smelled him, the thin layer of sweat coating his skin, felt his hot fingers on my skin. I wanted to roll my face over him, dig into his dense chest.

He was alert, thick and hard. His cock was alive between his legs, pre-cum dripping from the tip as his body felt the energy of the red. He was powerful and he made me powerful.

I realized that my breasts were dripping again, leaving trails of milk down my belly. They felt tingly and I knew that I could fall into that feeling if I wanted to. Cerrone dropped one hand and felt the blood from inside her in a pool between her legs. In the red, she stood up, covered in it. Her breath was was quick and she seemed made of animal energy as she painted her hands with blood and waved them over the bodies in front of us, spread out behind Savi. The air danced with her blood in arching ribbons, defying gravity with each arc upward,   and the scent of her built up around us warm and soft, like a kind of incense that was alive and precious and rare.

I could see in her now, in her belly. It was her gift and she controlled it. She was always pregnant. She was always ready to birth worlds from deep inside her. Tears fell down Maya's face as she realized that she belonged here, too.

This was her place, too.

Savi started and his eyes shot up, filled with red light. And every black, empty body around him woke up, alive, aware, painted with the blood of freedom.

5:20 PM

Vero Kaine took to the mic. He looked somehow bigger now, on the podium, in front of the microphone.

"Men. Today, I'm going to do something that the media hasn't done for you in a long long time. I'm going to tell you truths that you deserve.

Truths that you need to hear."

The audience grumbled, milled around. So many had no context for this. But it was coming.

"For the last 50 years, LifeQuest, the company you see beside you, has found a war on your behalf, a war complete with truly evil enemies and heroic soldiers fighting and dying on your behalf, on secret shores. I won't name names or organizations, but there are groups of women who have worked in secret to undermine you."

A smattering of applause came from the audience as they moved in, listening in earnest.

"Men. What would you say if I told you that we have worked tirelessly for fifty years to reverse the efforts of these women's groups to phase you out? What would you say if we made it clear that this is the line? Here. And we are drawing it now. Men are here to stay."

The men assembled broke into applause.

"I have men here on this stage who have been literally changed into biological women through the actions of these women, against their will."

The men began booing and yelling out.

"You heard from one yesterday. And you'll hear from more today."

Wild applause as the men surged forward, angry, confused.

"But first. I want you to see something. Something terrifying."

Med in LifeQuest uniforms pushed a cylinder forward. It was nearly filled with liquid, And floating in it was slight pinkish woman, struggling to keep her head above the liquid. She was nude and her head had been shaved. She looked poorly fed.

She looked terrified.

"Gentleman, this is Melan Orande. She is 24 years old, a Citizen of the great state of North California. A mutation, known as a Azoospermatix."

He stepped into it, tryng to conjure wonder. "Why is she known as that, my friends? Why is LifeQuest so engaged in finding people like this, people changed by the lie spread by women's groups. Because this Azoospermatix is grossly powerful."

He crossed in front of the cylinder, carrying the microphone with him.

This woman. This enemy of humanity carries with her a unique skill. One touch of her fingers, One breath, inhaling her air from her lungs, just a brush against her can render a man permanently and irrevocably sterile."

The audience booed and yelled out, pushing against the stage.

"This is what we are dealing with, men. These are people that can take you"—he pointed into the crowd—"or you, or you, out of the equation, with a casual brush of their hand against yours on the bus. Is that what you want?"

The crowd screamed out, surging forward. They pushed against the front of the stage. The stage began to shift and sway, almost like the deck of a ship. The cylinder shifted forward, tipping over into the crowd. It slammed to the ground and rolled over before smashing.

The woman inside fell out. She tried to stand, to protect herself against the raging crowd, moving like one solid mass. She lifted her hands in the air, bloody from the shattered glass that rose up like a ragged ring around her, and screamed.

The crowd washed over her.

And tore at her like animals.

5:30 PM

Meijo jumped up and ran to center stage. He couldn't see where the cylinder had gone or the woman inside it.

The crowd was flowing under the stage like a tide of people and the overhang obscured the light just enough to keep him seeing beneath them.

He called out. He jumped over the edge of the stage where he thought the cylinder had fallen. He fell to the ground and felt a boot against his head. He spread his hands, in search of Melan Orande. Finally, he found her arm and warpped his hand around it.

He pulled himself toward her and tried to climb on top of her. Half of the men looked like they were beating her—wrapped in shirts and sweaters, jackets, whatever material they could find—while the other half struggled to get away from her. Meijo wrapped himself around her and their fists pummeled his head as he lifted her up.

"Get away. It's not safe. I'm the only one who can safely touch her." He tried to appeal to their reason. A punch landed on his right temple.

"'Please. Get away. I'm trying to help you." He covered her up, fielding their punches.

His arms pulled her in close. He tried to make himself as big as possible. He felt a foot kick him between the legs and another in the face as he pulled her stage right. If he could get her out of the way of this thick morass of crowd, he might be able to find some protection. The kicks came down harder now as he fell, covering her up and pleading with the men to stop.

He crawled, the woman under him. He wanted to stop to see if she was ok, but he couldn't. He begged her to hang in there, under his breath, whispering into her ear, hoping she could hear him. Like an animal he crawled, broken rocks from the street ripping into his knees and elbows, fists coming down on every part of his body.

Suddenly, it stopped. He looked up to see an arm extended. On it was a Senza Dolore tattoo.

"It's ok. I've got her. I have her." He couldn't see the woman's face. He took a deep breath and lifted Melan Orande into her arms.

And passed out in the street.

5:35 PM

A wave of women poured into the open street. There must have been almost two hundred of them. They were armed with knives and more than held their own as the men descended on them. The undercurrent of violence had broken open now. The stage tipped finally and fell, with the occupants jumping off to one side or the other. Vero Kaine held onto the mic, inciting the men to push forward, to remove the women from the street,

He pointed to them and called them by name this time.

And the men assembled knew they were the enemy.

5:37 PM

Rana closed the refrigerator, pulling out cheese to make a light snack for Mia. She was used to spending time with Mia. Today she wondered if she hadn't messed up everything by being less than forthcoming with Cerrone. In relationships you never really know what's going to push it over the edge, like a piece of cheese sliding off a countertop. What's the thing that going to make it hard to wake up together tomorrow?

She knew she loved her. And she loved Mia. She grabbed the plate and a glass and decided that this wouldn't be it.

She stepped toward the bedroom and saw Mia standing in the doorway. Her eyes were lit up a deep crimson and her hands reached out to her. Rana gasped and dropped the glass in her hand.

Mia's voice seemed different. It was blogger, somehow, amplified.

She was speaking for her but also for something else. "They need you."

Mia lifted her hand to her and Rana took it. She had no idea what this was. But she trusted the little girl. Their hands connected and the light in the room shifted.

Rana closed her eyes.

5:40 PM

Bodies began to stream out the doors of lifequest. But these didn't bear any resemblance to the bodies pooling in the street, battling for inches of ground.

These were the bodies of gods. Men and women, some nude, some dressed in black underwear, new to the world, newly aware, seeing the sun willfully with their own eyes for the first time. And with them, Rik, Tanya, Eiko and Emmi, guiding them.

Most of the bodies were able to leave out the back doors, avoiding the riot, but a few hundred spilled out, connecting with the riot growing in the street, confusing matters even more. The Senza Dolore were ready for something like this but the men, gathered to hear news they weren't remotely prepared for today, were just terrified, panicked, Had they had a few minutes to think, many of them, I'm sure, would have been rational and calm and would have tried to figure out what this all meant.

But they didn't.

The men moved on to the lifeQuest bodies. Were these also strange deadly mutations? Could they change you into a woman with a kiss, drive you insane, make you sterile with just a breath from their lips? The men were terrified.

And they fought.

I looked across from me in the red to see Rana now, next to Maya. her eyes were wide as she took in everything she saw. I could tell by her breathing she was unprepared. She looked to me for answers and I tried to smile at her calmly, gently. Maya reached over and kissed her, kissing her eyes one at a time. She looked back, crystal clear, alive, her dark olive skin reflecting the glittering red of far away fires as Cerrone sat down again next to her, hand in hers.

"This isn't right. They're killing each other. This isn't what we wanted." she looked into Cerrone's face and begged.

Cerrone took her blood and splashed it across the air, it hung in place, thick and rich and began to shift, moving to display the scene below. Men were gathering weapons, trying to attack what they could. The women of the Senza Dolore were fighting back. We saw a woman stab a ruddy red faced man in the neck. I panicked, not seeing Meijo anywhere. My heart was pounding twice as fast as it ever had,

We reached out.

The sky shifted to red as we expanded our world into this other, less visceral one. Snakelike, red tendrils fell from the sky, wrapping themselves around the Senza Dolore, speaking to them in old languages that only bodies know, pushing them to grab the LifeQuest bodies and retreat.

They began to move, almost as one piece, dodging the men around them, pulling the bodies free, retreating backward, taking them with.

Hundreds of men now stood in the street, their skin illuminated by the viscous red washing across the sky. Tendrils spun down around them and stalked them, pressing against them, wrapping around them.

I looked to Maya and she smiled. She stood up now and lifted her hands into the mass of red tendrils above us like living, meaty ivy growing faster than humanly possible.

She was in charge now.

On the ground, Stephan Masconi felt the rhythms of the red rising up around him. He suddenly remembered a kiss from years ago, stolen in the middle of the night with his best friend James, and that memory of closeness rose up again in his chest pushing him forward. He almost slipped on the newly slick ground and steadied himself, leaning into Jonny Salci, someone he knew, just a bit, from the neighborhood. Without a doubt, as he felt the ribbon of muscle in his back, he wanted to know him better. He leaned in and pressed his face against Jonny's back, pulling his shirt up and wrapping his hands around him. From here he could feel Jonny's cock, throbbing through his jeans, and he had never felt something so raw and vibrant and desirable. He slipped off his belt and pulled his pants down, wrapping his hands around jonny's erect cock and playing with his balls as he pressed his lips against the delicate downy ridge of dark hair streaming from his back down his ass, ending in his perfect asshole.

Stephan kissed it slowly and felt Jonny moan beneath him. His cocked jumped in Stephan's hands and he spread himself, opening up for Stephan's wandering tongue. Jonny had never thought that he could want to be touched so badly but in the rich red light he knew this was right.

Closer to the stage, Ben Turner, still emotionally crushed over his wife's leaving just a week ago turned to see the most beautiful face he'd ever seen. Where Ben was dark and nearly hairless, this man, Anthony Spirini, was light skinned with a beard that tickled Ben 's face perfectly when he leaned in to kiss him that first time, their hands both exploring the other's body. Ben laughed at the sensation and pulled down Anthony's pants, anxious to see if the rich black pelt was everywhere. His heart leapt when he saw Anthony's sleek long cock rising up from a thick black bush. Ben felt its weight in his hand as he spread Anthony's legs with his knee and prepared to make love to him.

Anthony pulled him down on top of him, whispering to him to be his first, angling his ass toward Ben's pulsing black cock.

And when Ben finally bore down hard into Anthony's root, the lighter man let out a sigh of relief, of pleasure, pulling him in closer, into himself, trying to make it last but anxious for Ben's climax, hoping it would fill him completely, full of this man he just found.

All across the street, hundreds of men fell into each other, learning about each other, touching each other. Roland Ostrowski felt the animal drive to release as he dug his cock into Mark Jackson's open mouth. Mark wrapped his hands around Roland, silently waiting for the rush of his cum pouring down his throat, connecting him to the man he wanted so badly.

And Mako Olivo, still hurting from his breakup three months ago with the girl of his dreams, found a new dream in Tomi Molares, a man he worked with and never imagined he could feel this free with, this open, this passionate as they kissed there, right on the ground, massaging each other's cocks and whispering to each other, laughing, alive, in love in ways they never considered before, watching the riot wind down and fall into the red, earthy, musky, full of what makes your skin dance when the breeze drifts cross it in a completely new way.

5:52 PM

The Riot had stopped but what had replaced it was entirely alien to Vero Kaine. He suspected, though, that it was something unnatural.

In his mind.

He slid from the stage and gathered his guards. As they moved toward the side entrance of LifeQuest, he saw Meijo laying there on the ground, He grabbed his arm and lifted.

No matter what, he would prove this.

6:02 PM

My breathing was quick and raw. I'd never been in the Red world for so long. I started to feel myself falling. The street was littered with men moving together in physical excess, Alive, but lost in each other. I didn't know how to get out.

I thought of Meijo and let myself fall back onto the white.

Zoesis

I woke up on the floor of the soundstage inside LifeQuest.

Behind the soundstage, Vero Kaine stood there with his own personal army of about 20 men to one side with Miejo on the other. My heart filled up just seeing Meijo.

But not like this.

Kaine looked at me. I was in the white world again. He could see me, I was exhausted but my body was tingling all over. Part of me wanted to stay crouched on the ground like an animal.

"I remember you, bitch." Kaine laughed, "That poor boy. He didn't do anything. You know what his great crime was, that 12 year old boy? Michael? He liked you. He really liked you."

"I didn't mean it." I looked up at him. I knew my sheepish demeanor would make him talk. It was nearly impossible to keep it up, though. That was the longest time I'd ever been in the red world. I felt sweaty and wild. I felt my body leading me and it was intense. I wanted to grab Meijo and hold him. I wanted to explode. I wanted. It was hard to remember who I was.

But him? He was a classic bully.

"And after kissing all day in the backyard, he made the mistake of putting his finger in you, just one finger. " Kain held up a finger as if to illustrate.

"It's not something I can control." I felt that lack of control build. I realized I was breathing hard. I tried to calm myself.

"And you ruined his life," he continued.

The sight of Meijo standing there, head down, was inflaming me. He was hurt. His face was all black and blue. But I was tortured, too, emotionally. I knew what I did to him. "Stop it."

Kaine took a step toward me. Suddenly, I could see Rik at a side glass door, trying to get through so everyone else could be here. But that was going to take a minute. Maybe a minute too long. "He paid for that one moment for the rest of his life. And now, so will this one."

And Vero Kaine pointed to Meijo.

"You removed my memory." I pleaded. My head was swirling with all these animal impulses, but I had to keep him talking.

"We tried to learn from you and stop you, but it's unstoppable. All of it is."

I took a deep breath and looked at him confused. He would talk if he thought I was stupid. I just felt like pouncing. I felt alive and wily, trying to pretend i was stupid.

"There was another one like you, the exact same mutation. She was a stripper. She knew exactly what she was doing. We had to put her down." Kaine stepped down from the stage and approached her, taking a pulse gun from the holster of one of his soldiers.

You killed her?

"Others, different ones, too. Did you know there are about 36 different mutation types that have arisen on this planet, each one with the sole agenda of eliminating men." He tried to look menacing. And it was working. But why not me?

"Why didn't you kill me?" I advanced toward him. I was starting to come down, but there was so much energy in me.

"We studied you, we used what we found to make things, to bring us closer to a solution. To buy us time. And this company became very rich." Meijo and the rest of his soldiers followed him toward me, off the stage. I tried not to focus on Meijo there, although I could feel him in the room. If I closed my eyes, he would be all I could feel. I wanted his arms around me. I wanted to swallow him, my mouth on him.

The glass broke and Rik and the others tried to use the leverage to push the door in. He only had a minute or so. The soldiers in back turned toward the door.

"I'm not doing it on purpose," I yelled out, hoping to pull attention to me.

He was yelling now. "Of course you aren't. And neither are they, the other ones. Even that Melan Orande woman. But there is a war on men and you and your kind are waging it with your own biology. You fight in that war every minute with your bodies. None of us want to be here, fighting, do we?" His voice rose even higher.

"I'm sorry," Meijo dropped his head. Kaine turned to him Looking back at me he fired the gun over my head to rattle me.

"Do you know what a Thanarseniken is? It's a woman whose touch causes men to break down and die? There are four of those we've found. How about a Thilikogen? Their bodies kill male children in the womb. Kill them. We've found thirteen of them."

"And you eliminate them all?"

He took aim with the gun, directly at my head this time. "Yes, and you would, too. If it meant survival of your people."

Meijo pulled out the small phone-like device. "You aren't my people." Suddenly the wall behind Kaine lit up with the scene we were in. With him in front. It was video.

"What?"

Rik yelled out, from behind the guards, but I couldn't hear what he said.

Meijo looked at Kaine. "And the people watching this can decide if you're theirs."

Vero Kaine pointed his gun at Meijo in disgust. "Idiot. I was going to use all of our resources to help you. To get you back. Now you can just go fuck yourself, woman." He spat that last out as an insult.

Kaine dropped his shoulder and prepared to fire. The guard closest to him split off and came barreling forward, jumping in front of the gun. A hole opened in his chest, right over his heart. He fell over, still protecting Meijo.

"No," I cried out.

Maiejo tried to cover him up. He pulled off the mask.

It was Savi. He had snuck back to disguise himself as a guard.

"You shot him." Meijo looked up at him, tears welling up in his eyes.

Kain looked up, "That moronic body got in the way."

Meijo tried to pull the shirt off to see the damage. "Savi... Jees." There was a massive hole in his chest. He'd been so close to the gun.

Kaine waved the gun around. "What do you care? He's a man, right? The body is a man."

"C'mon. Savi." Meijo grabbed my hand and tried to put pressure on the wound along with me. But blood was pouring out of his chest. Despite all of it, touching Meijo's hand sent electrical jolts through me. We tried to stop the bleeding. My head was all over the place. I could smell everyone around me, feel them all. The chaos was bouncing off my skin in electric waves.

Meijo yelled at Kaine, "Fix him. Like you did with Mika. Fix him. You can..."

"No. And People will understand." Kaine went to put the gun back in the holster he'd taken it from.

The guard grabbed his hand. "No. They won't."

He looked at the hand as though in disbelief. "What are you doing?"

"Stopping you. This is a citizen's arrest." The other men turned to Kaine and pulled their guns.

"Fuck you. You're fired. You're all fired. Get off my property. " He tried to wrench his hand away, yelling at the men.

The guard was calm and repeated, "You're under arrest for murder and attempted murder."

Kaine's face went red as he screamed, spitting across the room, "Get the fuck off my property."

Rana pushed her way past the men who were putting handcuffs on Kaine. She pressed her hands on Meijo's. She had medical training.

I leaned down. "Please, Savi. Please stay. You haven't even barely had the chance to *do* anything yet. There is so much. Please. There's so much…" I reached out.

I closed my eyes and felt Cerrone kneel next to me. We held hands and tried to open our minds into the red. Maybe we could heal his body there. I pressed my eyelids together and saw the redness spreading but it was too much, in too short a period of time. We were raw. But she was there, next to me, sitting cross legged, the flickering fire playing off her brilliant onyx skin.

Across from us, we could see him, brown and sleek and full of everything good that people carried. We were all beautiful here. Sitting here with us, Savi was complete. He was part of the pantheon, part of everything. He was a total person. I could feel the part of him that I was mother to, and I know Cerrone could, too. I remembered releasing him with my blood weeks ago and thought how he had done so much good with his now.

I wrapped my arms around him just as I did out there, in the real world. I tried to funnel everything in me.

And when he died, we felt it out here and in the red world.

We felt it everywhere.

The world went white in a shock and suddenly the sound of everything hit me on all sides.

"You still owe me 20,000 dollars."

I looked up. Bron was standing above us. He was actually holding out his hand. I tried to stand.

"Oh, I forget, your girlfriend over here said to double it if I set you guys up here and played AV club."

Meijo had woken him up, back at my place, and convinced him to help record Kaine at this event. When he finally messaged me about it my heart went soaring. I knew he didn't just run off. But I also knew it was a full time job managing this idiot. We couldn't have done the broadcast without his help, but this was shitty timing. I didn't hate Bron, but I felt brutalized inside. I couldn't think. There were tears pouring down my face.

I stood up and fished the envelope out of my pocket. "You want money?"

"I just want what I'm owed. Then I never see you freaks again."

That sounded good to me. So good. I threw the envelope, without counting it. It scattered across the room as the white washed everywhere. I fell back down, slipping in Savi's blood, and just felt stupid and weak and wanting. I put my head in my hands while he slowly picked money up off the ground.

Some of it was covered in blood and that seemed appropriate. The alarm was going off now and it was so loud.

I think I just screamed and waited for it to stop.

Epilogue 1

And that's what the world saw on that recording.

Right before I fell apart.

A group of men standing up to Vero Kaine and taking him into custody for his campaign against women. A man sacrificing himself for a woman. Four women working so hard to save that man, mourning him, crying over him. They saw Rana with her Senza Dolore tattoo with tears in her eyes, trying to bring him back.

this wasn't the riot, simplistic and full of confusion. These were people with time to act like who they were. And it wasn't even the incredibly confusing mass gay orgy that ended the Riot, one that left so many people with enduring feelings and ways of looking at things.

It was a moment. And it hurt, in a lot of ways. It wasn't fixing or solving anything but it meant something. It meant compassion for each other in a world that had had too little of that for too long. It meant that men and women here were able to make themselves part of the same story, no matter what biology had to say about it. It meant change.

It was the lesson of the orange cat all over again. It was how a small moment could tell a big story that people wanted and waited for. One that went on forever.

Maya's powers are permanent, it seems. Under the influence of her abilities, the most intense of the rioters became bisexual.

And that intensity translated into passion, into a deep body need.

Most of the news outlets couldn't figure it out so they didn't talk about it much. And when people found out, by word of mouth, well, it made rioting a bit more complicated. I saw a magazine article that was titled, "Does Rioting Make you Gay?" Hard hitting stuff.

I'm told that there are less than half the number of men on the planet today than there are women. Now, everything is sort of out in the open. Men have been in the minority for a while, due to violence, aggression, a million things that their behavior has brought home to them. Experts say now that, given the new circumstances, the equilibrium may really end up being 15:1 with fifteen times the number of women on the planet than men. I don't know what that means for trans men. I don't know what it means for intersex people. Honestly, biology is messy as Rik likes to say.

At that point, men will become novelties. I suspect that the men who experience that will find it interesting. At the very least. It could well be that being a "man" becomes something that people are openly willing to culturally create. And maybe we only lose some of what is at the far end of the biologial continuum.

None of us know what is coming next, now that the planetary bios is changing. Famous pundit Aria Xavani says that the planet may have needed men, in its earlier stages. And now that they are no longer needed, it's been brutal about eliminating them. The ecosystem can do that, apparently.

Scientists have found seven more evolutions that have been occurring, making men obsolete, bringing the grand total up to forty-three. No one is hiding them anymore. Everyone seems to be working together to make it easier for the men who are still here. Ironically, the Senza Dolore have been effective in making sure that men are not hurt, as they become more and more of a minority. They've always been about the underdog, as men are discovering.

Men, for their part, are coming face to face with a reality that can't be wished away.

The evolutions are so prevalent now that no one can pretend they aren't happening. There is a reason why biology has dictated this course of action, It's being called the Zoesis, which means the moment when an ecological system is optimized to support and promote the life that is in it.

The riots went on for two weeks . Then they slowed down. Then they just disappeared. men stopped hunting women with the mutations. It was big. too big to fight. and inarguable. And, I confess, we showed up at some of them. Maya was helpful. In Oregon, there is an Idemomorph, too, and she showed up at a couple of riots.

No one can pretend that women aren't safer without men around. No one can pretend that men haven't been violent, destructive, deadly to a planet that originally welcomed them. No one can deny any of this. It's just something that has to be faced head on.

And we're facing it.

Epilogue 2

Meijo, Emmi and I were married a few months later. Some days he dresses and acts like Meijo and sometimes, well, sometimes not. It all depends on how he feels inside.

Or how she feels.

And that has added a lot of fun to our everyday routine, honestly. I'm grateful that we still have what we had. That I still have them. They make sure I don't feel bad for what I've taken away.

For what I am.

Meijo and I had been in contact while trying to get to Vero Kaine to speak out publicly since the message in the hallway. We thought it might be our best bet at figuring this all out. He was never really mad at me and he was never really a hostage. Sure, he might have been upset and confused by the situation, but he tells me he never really wanted to be away from me.

And I know that people can't really fix each other, but to hear him say that... Well. It reached into my head and pulled out some bad things. He changed me as much as I changed him. And Emmi chose us both.

So, we wanted to make sure we all tied the knot before it happened.

Before our Savi was born. It turns out you can get pregnant the very first time you actually have sex.

He's a beautiful baby boy, bright, happy. He looks so much like Miejo. And he loves having three doting parents. He's so alive and kind of brilliant. And he seems immune to whatever it is that I do to turn men into women. We know because it was a natural birth. And it was beautiful.

But he's definitely immune. Just like the other Savi was.

Just like my friend was.

So are the rest of the Lifequest bodies. So far, over 3,000 of them have been liberated in ten different states. Cerrone and I have been able to "switch them on," one at a time, or in groups, bringing them to consciousness.

And no one will use them again like that.

But most other people are susceptible to what happens when they have sex with me. There is something in my vaginal mucosa that triggers it. And it can't be reversed. It breaks down the Y chromosome and creates a kind of androgen insensitivity afterward. I can't control it.

It seems to work in just a few hours.

I don't have a trust fund anymore, but we do ok. We moved back into the house and people visit us. Some people come to hear stories. Some people come to change. Women who were born in male bodies. Men who don't want to be men anymore.

People with their own reasons.

I have sex with some of them and some of them I treat, using what I have.

There are people who visit Maya, too. Her abilities are distributed by pheromones, so it's a lot harder to control. I've seen her do it, now. Not just like what she did at the riot. I've seen her take a song and slow dance with someone and change them.

Forever.

And I try to talk to men about what they really want. I turn some people away. Some men are fixated on not being needed anymore. It's a big hit to the ego, I know.

Luna and Tee stay with us when they can. There is a world for them to explore. Luna has my sense of humor and Emmi's whimsy. It's fascinating to watch. Tee is leading the union of Secondbodies working to get full personhood from the new government. She's pretty amazing.

I've spent more time in the Red World. Cerrone, Maya, and I all have. We discover that Mia can send people there. I haven't managed to use it again quite like I did that day, but we haven't even begun to explore it in there. It seems endless and I have a sense that we could do a lot more in there than we understand now.

I feel like there are answers in there and I want to find them, but I know it's going to take time.

I'm willing to be patient.

What does it mean if we are all connected, all part of one body? Maybe all of our exploring and playing and finding new ways to touch and love each other are ways to find that connection and what we can do with it?

Talking to Rik, I had wondered out loud if the planet ever really needed any of us. We agreed that maybe needing us wasn't the point. I mean, Cerrone doesn't NEED Rana to have a child, but she's going to do it again soon, anyway.

She's going to give Mia a little sister. And Rana will be right there.

Even I myself have been so immersed in the economy of need, feeling the ideology of need, pursuing the methods of need. I thought I needed so many things. I may have been missing something big.

What does it matter if the planet doesn't need us? So, what does it matter if the human race doesn't need men anymore?

What does it matter if we aren't needed at all. Any of us?"

Rich, poor, fat, thin, beautiful, old, weak, sad, afraid, disabled, gifted, neurotypical, spectrummy, lost, found, all of us.

When do any of us feel needed all the time?

Emmi says she thinks that we can build a world where maybe none of us are needed.

A world where every one of us is just wanted.

And I think that maybe that's going to be better.

SECONDBODY

BY LIFEQUEST

www.ingramcontent.com/pod-product-compliance
Lightning Source LLC
Chambersburg PA
CBHW051340020726
47501CB00007B/2197